KEEP ME FROM HARM

Carol Oliver came to Barcelona to meet the man she loved, but found herself betrayed to a gang of ruthless kidnappers. A family friend, John Oldfield, had been sent to put an end to her unsuitable romance, but instead the two of them found themselves on the run in the wild hills of Spain. Even greater danger threatened them back in Barcelona. What they had to endure in order to survive taught them a lot about themselves and about each other.

SHEILA HOLROYD

KEEP ME FROM HARM

Complete and Unabridged

LINFORD
Leicester

First published in Great Britain in 2004

First Linford Edition
published 2005

British Library CIP Data

Holroyd, Sheila
    Keep me from harm.—Large print ed.—
Linford romance library
    1. Love stories
    2. Large type books
    I. Title
    823.9'14 [F]

    ISBN 1–84395–707–8

Published by
F. A. Thorpe (Publishing)
Anstey, Leicestershire

Set by Words & Graphics Ltd.
Anstey, Leicestershire
Printed and bound in Great Britain by
T. J. International Ltd., Padstow, Cornwall

This book is printed on acid-free paper

1

Dusk had fallen in Barcelona, but Carol could see the hotel's illuminated sign a little distance ahead as she walked along the narrow side street in the city's old town. She was excited by the adventure she had begun that day, and so deep in her plans for the future that she did not spare a glance for the two youths walking towards her.

They separated as they reached her, passing on either side, then without warning one pushed her violently towards the other youth who grabbed the leather strap of her shoulder bag, nearly pulling her off her feet.

Shocked and unbelieving, Carol clung to her bag and drew in a breath to scream for help, but the first youth clamped a hand over her mouth. She struggled hard enough to dislodge his hand, which she promptly bit, prompting a stream of Spanish curses as he seized her again.

Then she heard the sound of a car opening and an angry shout as a figure raced along the pavement and suddenly hurtled into the bag-snatcher, knocking him to the ground. The other youth released Carol as he turned to face this unexpected challenge. She tried to leap over the fallen man, her eyes on the safety of her hotel such a short distance away, but he caught at her foot and she went sprawling on the pavement.

As she lay winded, gasping for breath, she could hear the dull impact of body blows and then a yelp of dismay. There was the sound of running feet, and as she pulled herself up to a sitting position, the fallen youth scrambled up and ran after his vanishing friend at top speed, leaving her bag lying on the ground.

Her rescuer was leaning against the wall, holding his head. She seized her bag and tucked it under her arm then approached him cautiously, resisting the urge to run away.

'Are you all right?' she asked nervously.

'No!' the bitter and forceful reply came in English. 'I've just been hit with something very hard.'

He took his hand away from his head and peered at her.

'Have you suffered any damage?'

She realised she felt shocked and shivery, but shook her head.

'I may have a few bruises, but that's all, fortunately. And they didn't get my bag.'

The stranger fumbled in his pocket and brought out a handkerchief with which he gingerly dabbed at his head before inspecting the result.

'Well, I'm bleeding, but not too badly,' he decided, and his attention returned to Carol.

'I don't know who you are,' she said as she prepared to thank her unknown rescuer, but he interrupted her.

'I'm pretty sure I know who you are.

You're Carol Oliver, aren't you?' I'm John Oldfield and I've been parked here for some time waiting for you to show up.'

A moment before, Carol had been a picture of grateful concern, but now she stepped back as if her rescuer had suddenly turned into a snake that threatened to bite her.

'You!' she said in horror. 'Leave me alone! You'll spoil everything!'

Turning, she gripped her bag and hurried in the direction of the hotel, only to feel John Oldfield's hand on her arm.

'We've got to talk!' he said urgently.

'No, we don't. I have nothing to say to you.'

He fell into step beside her, and as she reached the entrance to the hotel he stood in front of her, his tall figure blocking her way, and tried again.

'Look, I've just saved you from robbery or worse. You owe me something in return. Just give me a few minutes.'

In the harsh light of the doorway she looked at him hesitantly. A trickle of blood was running down the left side of his face from his fair hair. When he saw her looking at it he grimaced and wiped it away with his handkerchief, wincing as he touched his head.

'I need a cup of coffee, badly. Come with me. Surely you can stand my company for half an hour.'

A shaky smile crossed her face.

'I could do with a coffee, too, I suppose, but shouldn't we do something about your head first?'

'It's only a flesh wound. I'll have a nasty bruise tomorrow, but I'll survive.'

He took her arm and started walking back along the street.

'We'll take my car to a place I know. I promise to bring you back here, if you want to come,' he finished, casting a disapproving look back at the flaking paint of the hotel doorway and the narrow, uncarpeted entrance hall.

* * *

His elegant little car took them to a café in a quiet street. The owner looked up sharply as the pair entered, saw the bloodstained face, and decided he could do without such patrons. He advanced to block their entrance, but John Oldfield strode in with arrogant assurance, assumed the man was coming to welcome them, and issued orders for two large cups of coffee as he ushered Carol towards a booth which gave at least an impression of privacy. The owner saw at a second glance the expensively casual clothes and decided that as it was too late to keep them out he might as well accept their custom and the coffee arrived quickly.

Carol looked at her companion and gave a tremulous laugh.

'I wouldn't have let us in.'

He raised an eyebrow.

'You've still got blood smeared all over one side of your face,' she pointed out.

The handkerchief came into play again, but he grinned at her a little maliciously.

'Of course he could also have objected to the fact that your top is filthy and so are your jeans, which also happen to have one knee ripped. In fact, you look a real mess.'

She looked down at her clothes with horror, realising for the first time just how much of Barcelona's dirt had clung to her.

'Let's agree neither of us looks our best,' John Oldfield said, pushing the sugar bowl towards Carol.

'I don't take sugar,' she informed him coldly.

'It might be a good idea to have some now, to help combat the shock you've had.'

As she ignored his suggestion, he unwrapped a lump of sugar, dipped it in his coffee and then popped it in his mouth, crunched and swallowed. He gave Carol a grin that made him look as if he were a schoolboy instead of in his mid-twenties.

'I used to love dipping sugar in my mother's coffee when I was a child. I still find it very comforting in emergencies.'

Carol regarded him with prim disapproval for some seconds, then gave into temptation and unwrapped a lump and dipped it in her cup. Following his example, she crunched and swallowed, and found the coffee-flavoured sweetness very comforting. She repeated the process.

'I think my mother would disapprove,' she said guiltily, hesitating with her fingers poised above the sugar bowl for a third time.

'Well, you were brought up much more strictly than I was.'

She drank some coffee and a tinge of colour returned to her white cheeks. She put her cup down and folded her hands in her lap and looked across the table.

'Go on then,' she said resignedly. 'Give your little speech. I'm sure you have one ready, if I know my parents.'

He frowned at her, then shrugged.

'I have got a speech prepared,' he

confirmed. 'In fact I took a lot of trouble composing it. But I'm beginning to wonder if it is appropriate after all.'

She looked at him enquiringly.

'I was sent here,' he went on, 'to bribe, persuade or threaten your boyfriend so that he would go away and leave you alone.'

She had picked up her cup again, but now set it down so hastily that some of the liquid splashed out into the saucer.

'What boyfriend? What are you talking about?'

If there was an apprehensive note in her voice John did not seem to hear it. He sighed wearily.

'Don't you realise that your parents are convinced that you have run away because you have fallen for some man who is so unsuitable that you dare not tell them about him?'

Little did he know how nearly right her parents were!

'What makes them think I've got a boyfriend? Where is this unsuitable man?' she spluttered defensively.

'I was beginning to wonder if they had got their facts straight,' her companion went on. 'You were on your own in the street, there didn't seem to be anybody at the hotel you wanted to rush to for comfort, and you haven't tried to telephone anyone to tell them what happened to you. Besides, Father said you were always guarded so carefully that he didn't think you ever had a chance to meet an unsuitable male.'

She felt safer now.

'You mean that just because I didn't do exactly what I was told for once, my family jumped to these sensational conclusions and you were sent to rescue me?'

He nodded and went on to explain.

'I was in Spain, working steadily at our offices in Bilbao, when suddenly I received an urgent call from England, from your father. Your mother had telephoned the hotel where they had reserved a room for you to see if you had arrived safely and was told you had sent the hotel's chauffeur away at the airport and hadn't been seen since.

'Then she heard that you hadn't disappeared completely but had taken leave of your senses and were staying in some sordid back-street hotel. I was then ordered into action. You know how the system works.'

She nodded. She had always known. Her father, James Oliver, had become friends with James Oldfield when they were both at Oxford and a few years later they had united their talents to form an import-export company which had gradually expanded into transport and communications.

Double O, as the company was affectionately known to their families, had made them both very rich. They had remained close friends as well as working partners but had chosen very different wives, with the result that the families rarely met.

She had last seen John Oldfield when he had been a lanky youth. However, in

11

an emergency it was taken for granted that any Oliver would do everything they could to help an Oldfield, and any Oldfield would do the same for an Oliver.

John put down his empty cup and studied Carol unobtrusively. Her short dark hair emphasised the pallor of her face, and there were shadows under her dark hazel eyes. In spite of that it was obvious that she was on the point of blossoming into a very attractive young woman. What a pity she was Carol Oliver!

'I'm hungry,' he told her. 'Would you like something to eat?'

'I'm not sure. I couldn't face a full meal.'

'Then let me introduce you to the great Spanish invention of tapas.'

He summoned the owner and conversed with him in fluent Spanish, and soon a waitress appeared with an assortment of little savoury snacks and a plateful of bread.

'You'll like this,' John assured a

dubious-looking Carol. 'Just eat what takes your fancy.'

John began to help himself from various dishes. After an initial hesitation, Carol tried first one little savoury and then another, and discovered that she was hungry after all. When the plates were empty John sat back.

'I hadn't eaten since lunchtime. How about you?'

'I had a hamburger,' Carol said proudly, 'with chips.'

'Did you enjoy it?'

She wrinkled her nose and shook her head.

'Not very much, in fact I left most of it, but would you believe it was the first time I've ever gone into a café by myself and ordered a meal.'

He looked at her pityingly.

'How old are you, Carol?'

'Eighteen.'

'And this was the first time you had ever bought yourself something to eat? We have been brought up differently! When I was eighteen, I was living on cheap snacks during the summer holidays and working for the money to pay for them.'

'I know. Mother disapproved strongly.'

'Father gave me one hundred pounds and told me to come back in two months' time. He thought it would teach me some valuable lessons about people and money if I had to support myself for a while, and I think he was right. Anyway, don't let's squabble about the past. If you haven't fallen desperately in love, why are you here staying in a cheap, back-street dive when your parents had reserved a room at the best hotel in the city for you?'

She hesitated, gazing at the table and wondering what it was safe to tell him, then she sat up straight and glared at him defiantly.

'I'm eighteen, yet I'm still protected and told what to do as if I were a child! I suppose most people would think I have a wonderful life. I'm looked after, I have the best of everything, and I don't have to worry about working for my living.

'Well, there are an awful lot of things that most girls of my age have done that I've never been allowed to do. So I decided it was time to experience life outside the world of the Olivers.

'I have just spent a couple of weeks with Mary Carter and her family on their yacht and my parents will be in Barcelona in a few days' time on business, so when the yacht called at Marbella I was put on a plane to Barcelona like a parcel, to wait here till they collected me. While I was on the plane I realised that there wasn't going to be anyone waiting in Barcelona who could tell me what to do. I had a chance to do something different. A chauffeur was waiting at the airport, ready to whisk me off to the hotel. You should have seen his face when I told him that he could take my luggage to the hotel but I wasn't going with him!'

'What did you do instead?'

'Sent him off with everything except my hand luggage which had the basics I need for a few days. I had my passport, plenty of money and some credit cards. I was sure I could manage.'

'What about that hotel you booked into?'

She looked smug.

'I bought a students' guide to Barcelona at the airport bookshop. It said that hotel was suitable for students, so I telephoned and booked a room and then took a taxi there from the airport. And I did telephone home so that my parents would know where I was.'

'I know. You gave the message to the housekeeper and ended the call before she could contact your mother! That was when our parents started telephoning each other, with the result that I've spent several hours driving across the country to rescue you, which I did, incidentally, though not from a lover, so my mission was not altogether in vain.'

Carol was congratulating herself. She had only told him half the truth, but he had accepted it. Now she had the grace to admit that he had not received the thanks he deserved.

'I am really very grateful that you appeared at that moment. Thank you for helping me,' she said very politely.

'Spoken like a well-brought-up young lady. Incidentally, what did you think of the hotel when you saw it? Was it a great shock? I wasn't very impressed when I asked for you there.'

'It is not what I am accustomed to, of course,' she said carefully, 'but I am sure it is adequate.'

She didn't tell him how horrified she had been by the shabby, little room, and how taken aback she had been to find that for the first time in her life she would not have her own bathroom!

'It's adequate for street-wise youngsters who know how to survive in a big city,' John Oldfield said crisply, 'but it's not suitable for you. It's a rough area, and you have already found out the hard way that there are plenty of thieves around looking for solitary victims.'

She shivered as she recalled those few

seconds of pure terror, but shook her head firmly.

'I am not going to that hotel my parents have chosen just to sit and wait until they arrive, and you can't make me. For once I intend to do what I want, so don't you try and tell me what to do.'

He held up a soothing hand.

'Don't get upset. Your mother may never forgive me, but I do have a lot of sympathy for you. In fact, I think it might be a good idea for you to escape from your privileged lifestyle for a few days, but there are some precautions which you must take if you are to survive till your parents get here.'

She glared indignantly but he stared her down.

'Remember, Carol, that if anything happens to you, every Oliver and every Oldfield will hold me to blame.'

This was true. She bit her lip and forced herself to listen to him.

'Firstly, I insist you move from that hotel to one in a safer area. When I did a few weeks' backpacking round Europe some years ago, I stayed at a little place just outside the old quarter. It's perfect for what you need and it's comfortable, too.

'I've sent friends there since, and the lady who runs the *hostal* knows me well enough to find you a room even at this late hour.'

'A hostel?' Carol said. 'You mean a youth hostel? I'm not going to one of those!'

'A *hostal*, you idiot. It's like a hotel, but with no public rooms and it doesn't provide meals, but it is clean and comfortable, and the lady is very kind and very helpful. Now I'm in Barcelona, I can get some work done for our firm before your parents come, but I can also spare some time to show you a little of the city and tell you how to get about, things like that.'

Carol summoned up a smile, even though she felt ready to lay her head on the table and fall asleep there and then. The day had been exhausting, physically and mentally.

'I'm sorry to have disrupted your schedule so unexpectedly, and I will be grateful for your help. I must admit that once I'd sent the chauffeur away there was a very nasty moment when I did begin to wonder if I could cope on my own. However, I don't need you to show me around. I'm not absolutely useless and incompetent. If I buy a guide I'm sure I can find the main tourist attractions.'

'I can arrange my timetable to suit you.'

'John, you've rescued me from muggers and you say you can find me a decent place to stay. That will be enough. Please let me have a chance to be a normal girl instead of an Oliver.'

He looked at her dubiously, and then his lips twitched.

'OK. I'll give you your freedom for a few hours tomorrow, but I'll meet you tomorrow evening and make sure you have a decent meal.'

He fumbled in his pocket and gave her a card.

'That's got my mobile phone number on it. I've been given yours. Now I'll telephone the *hostal*.'

There was a brief conversation in Spanish on his mobile phone, and then he slipped it back into his pocket and smiled at her.

'A room is waiting for you. Let's go back to my car and get your bag from that other place.'

This did not take long. The bored receptionist was not interested in a guest who decided to leave suddenly. Carol had already paid for the night, so if she chose to go off somewhere else with a young man, why should she bother?

Quickly, Carol collected her bag from the room where she had left it earlier and John Oldfield drove her from the narrow, twisted streets of the Gothic Quarter to the wide, nineteenth-century elegance of the Passeig de Gracia.

The *hostal* was above some expensive-looking shops and was reached by an impressive lift, all shining mirrors and polished wood. On the third floor, a small, lively middle-aged woman was waiting for them. She greeted John like an old friend, exclaimed with horror at his bloodstained hair, looked at Carol with open curiosity and spoke to John at length in rapid-fire Spanish. Something she said suddenly provoked John into obvious protest.

There was a lot of shrugging and eyebrow rising, but finally the lady seemed satisfied. She nodded briskly and picked up Carol's bag.

'The señora doesn't speak English, I'm afraid,' John explained to Carol.

'I realise that, but what exactly was the matter just then?'

He grinned widely.

'A slight misunderstanding, I'm afraid. She thought I intended to stay here with you tonight, as a couple. Anyway, I've explained the situation, and that my mission is in fact to protect your honour, and she has sworn to look after you like a mother.'

'One is enough,' Carol sighed, and got a sympathetic look. 'Where are you staying tonight?' she added.

'I've taken over the reservation at the luxury hotel you spurned. I intend to enjoy the luxury after my dash through Spain.'

He looked down on her tired face sympathetically.

'And incidentally, I do think you showed real courage in deciding to face the world on your own, even though I'm not quite sure you are ready to do so. I'll have to call your parents tonight to say I've contacted you and you are quite safe, but I won't tell them about the mugging or the sleazy hotel. That would have an awful lot of relatives flying into Barcelona tomorrow.'

She summoned up the energy to smile up at him gratefully and suddenly he bent and kissed her on the lips.

'Good-night, Carol Oliver. Enjoy your adventure.'

Then he was gone and the señora showed her into a comfortable, little bedroom with a tiny, private bathroom leading off it. Left to herself, she undressed, washed rapidly, and climbed gratefully between the cool fresh sheets.

She was exhausted, but too much had happened during the day for her to fall asleep instantly. She reviewed what had passed since that moment on the aeroplane when she had decided to disobey her parents and launch herself on her great adventure. They had almost guessed the truth, however, but fortunately her secret had not been discovered.

She would meet Juan tomorrow. It would depend on him whether she kept her date with John Oldfield or not.

2

Carol woke to find golden shafts of sun piercing the curtains and lighting the little bedroom. For a few minutes she lay still, looking round at the simple room furnished with sturdy but aging pieces of furniture.

This was the first full day of her new life, deciding for herself where to go and what to do. Admittedly, John Oldfield would be there waiting to help her if anything went wrong, and after her experience with the bag snatchers she was prepared to accept that she might need a little guidance, but he would not be the first person she would turn to. Juan would be there to help her.

Throwing aside the bedclothes, she made for the bathroom, where she gazed at her face in the mirror above the washbasin. The short black hair was tousled with sleep but her large eyes glowed with excitement. Carol studied her reflection. Was she pretty? Juan had looked at her as if she were more than pretty and had whispered 'beautiful' to her. Today she would find out if he had really meant it.

Carol washed and dressed rapidly and then hesitated. The *hostal* did not serve breakfast and she had a healthy appetite. What should she do? She emerged from her room shyly to find her hostess hovering outside the door. Carol was seized by the elbow and led to a window. In thirty seconds of vivid mime the message was conveyed that if Carol were to cross the road to the café the hostess was indicating, she would be able to enjoy a good breakfast there at a very reasonable price.

She then took Carol's shoulder bag and adjusted it so that the strap crossed the girl's breast, making it much more difficult for anyone to snatch it. Carol thanked her and made for the street.

A waiter in the café who knew just

enough English to cope with the menu provided her with orange juice, croissants and delicious coffee. When she left, she gave him a grateful smile. She was unsure how much of a tip she should give, but she gave him such an enormous one that the waiter hoped very much that the English girl would be staying at the *hostal* for a very long time!

She stood outside on the wide pavement and looked uncertainly at her watch. Was it too early to call Juan? She would spend an hour strolling round Barcelona, and then she would make that all-important call.

Following the tourist map she had acquired at the airport, she made her way to the enormous square where the ancient Gothic heart of Barcelona meets the elegant nineteenth-century streets. She found the wide, busy street leading down to the port, and strolled along it for a while.

She was glancing at her watch more and more frequently. Sinking down at a pavement table, she ordered a coffee. Very soon it would be time to call Juan. Her eyes grew dreamy as she remembered that first meeting with him. The Carters had arrived at their yacht together with a taxi carrying their luggage, and for a moment there had been chaos as the various suitcases were sorted out. Carol had claimed hers and then Mrs Carter had beckoned to one of the crew.

'Take Miss Oliver's bags and show her to her cabin,' she had ordered.

The dark-haired crew member, dressed in faded jeans and a white singlet, had picked up the suitcases and then turned to Carol. She became aware of dark eyes in a sun-tanned face, eyes that looked at her with sudden appreciation, and then he had smiled and gestured to her to follow him. Going below decks, she had been aware of the ease with which he managed the heavy suitcases, the muscles in his brown arms flexing.

When he had found her cabin and put down the cases, he had turned and smiled at her again and she saw that he was not much older than she was. For a moment she had wondered uneasily if he wanted a tip, but then he had moved closer to her.

'My name is Juan,' he said simply. 'I am at your service.'

Then he had moved smoothly past her and vanished along the passage-way.

For the rest of her time on the yacht she had been acutely aware of his presence, letting her eyes roam the deck with apparent casualness until she saw him. With her gaze shielded by her dark glasses, she had watched him, noting his grace and agility.

In the evening he had helped to serve dinner. It always seemed to be Juan who was there to draw out her chair, to be ready to offer her a serving dish or fill her glass, and at such moments they had looked at each other, emotions were conveyed without words. Sometimes they would pass each other below deck, and then she would be aware of his physical nearness and the softly-murmured compliment.

She had been very careful to keep her interest in him hidden from the Carters, afraid that daring to admire their young guest might cost the young man his job.

Carol had accepted resignedly that after they had reached Marbella she would never see him again, and had even been prepared to laugh at herself for being so fascinated by a handsome face and a few words when she knew nothing about him as a person. But then, on the last day, he had been the one who came to her cabin to collect her cases. Overcome by shyness, she had pointed to where they stood side by side, but instead of picking them up he had held out a small card to her.

'I have heard that you are going to Barcelona,' he murmured. 'So am I. That is my cousin's address, where I will be staying.'

As she gazed at him, surprised and bewildered, he took the cases and strode out, leaving her with her heart thumping. So his looks to her had meant something! He was as aware of her as she was of him and wanted to see her again, but he was leaving the decision whether to call him or not to her.

Desperately, as the plane had carried her northwards, she had tried to think how she could escape from supervision long enough to contact him in Barcelona. Once she was in the hotel she knew that her mother would have arranged for acquaintances to call and amuse her daughter by showing her the city. It was then she had realised that the airport gave her an opportunity to escape. The chauffeur did not have the authority to insist she went with him to the hotel.

She stirred and looked at her watch again. Finally, she decided, the time had come. She took out her mobile phone and dialled the number she had memorised so carefully. A voice she had never heard before answered, snapping out some phrase in Spanish.

'Juan?' Carol said carefully. 'Juan Sastre? Is he there?'

There was a brief pause, then, 'Momentito.'

Carol held on for a full minute till she heard another voice.

'Juan Sastre here.'

She closed her eyes, so full of delight and relief that she could hardly speak.

'It's Carol, Carol Oliver,' she stammered at last.

'Carol!'

He sounded amazed. Hadn't he believed that she would call him?

'I got here yesterday.'

She paused, wondering what to say next.

'And you called me!' his voice said triumphantly. 'How soon can we meet?'

'I am free at least until this evening, Juan. Where can I see you? I think there is a park not far away.'

'No! You must come here, to my home, and meet my family.'

Her heart sank. She had imagined

the two of them walking through the park together. The idea of being presented to a family gathering was much less appealing and much, much less romantic. But it did show serious intentions, didn't it?

'I suppose I could,' she said reluctantly, 'but how do I find you?'

'You still have the card I gave you? Show it to any taxi driver and he will bring you here. Find a taxi and we will be together in ten minutes.'

She assured him she would be there soon, and the call ended. However, she did not rush to summon one of the many taxis that passed, but sat with her cold cup of coffee, frowning slightly. Carol was an only child, carefully shielded from many of the harsh realities of life by wealth and influence, but she knew that what she was proposing to do was risky. To go to the home of a virtually unknown young man without telling anyone else what she was doing could be dangerous.

But to question Juan's trustworthiness was to question her own powers of judgment, to question whether what she felt was love or infatuation.

Ever since he had given her his address she had woven romantic dreams around him, scarcely acknowledging that they were based on a few smiles and muttered words. It was the first time Carol had felt like this, and she was unwilling to let harsh reality spoil it.

Finally she fumbled in her pocket for the little square of card, stood up with decision, walked to the edge of the pavement and signalled to a cruising taxi which drew up beside her.

But when she showed the card to the driver he looked sharply at her and frowned.

'You are sure? This is the right address?'

'Yes. What's the matter?'

'This is not a nice area, not a nice place. Not suitable for a young girl.'

At first she was ready to listen, but

then she rebelled. Here was yet another adult telling her what she should or shouldn't do, interfering with her life!

'Will you please take me there, or do I have to get another taxi?'

The driver shrugged. He had done his best to warn the girl and he didn't want to lose a fare. In a few minutes they were in a warren of small, dark streets, very different from the populous tourist areas, and the taxi drew up outside a small bar, its windows grimy and uninviting. The driver turned to Carol.

'This is the place. You sure you want to get out here?'

'You are certain this is the place?'

'Quite sure.'

She stared at the uninviting premises, very near to telling him to drive her back to the city. But it wasn't Juan's fault that he was poor and had to live in such a run-down area. She opened the door and got out, paid off the disapproving driver and pushed open the bar door before she could have second thoughts.

Inside, she faltered and came to a stop. The bar was dark, long and narrow and she had become the focus for the stares of the half-dozen men who sat on tall stools or lounged against the bar. All conversation ceased. The balding, middle-aged barman stopped wiping the counter and looked at her interrogatively. But at that moment the door at the end of the bar flew open and a young man hurried up to her and seized her hands.

'Carol!'

It was Juan, and she relaxed, breathing a sigh of relief. Everything would be all right now — but it wasn't.

The men at the bar had come back to life and were leering, making comments which drew coarse laughter from their friends. She was acutely conscious of this even as she was trying to digest the fact that Juan, the yacht's crew member, and Juan in Barcelona were very different.

Instead of jeans and a white singlet

he was wearing a shiny bright blue suit and his dark hair was glued down with gel. Even as she greeted him she was aware of the strong smell of cheap after-shave.

'I took a taxi, as you said,' was all she could think to say, but already he was drawing her along the bar and through the door at the back.

There was a final burst of comments and gestures from the customers, and Juan shouted something at them that produced raucous laughter.

'We can talk in my room,' he said, leading her up a narrow, dark stairway to the first floor, where he opened a door and tried to usher her in.

She halted on the threshold. It was a stale-smelling room, the bed unmade and the curtains still drawn.

'Come in,' Juan urged her, and she found herself sitting on the edge of the bed with Juan beside her, stripping off his jacket.

'I was not sure that you would call me,' he said soulfully. 'I thought your rich friends might stop you.'

'Oh, I managed to get away from them,' she stared, and then gabbled on, informing him what had happened since she came to Barcelona, while inside a small voice was telling her that she had made a dreadful mistake and must get away as soon as possible.

He listened while she told him about the chauffeur at the airport, and looked alarmed when she went on with an account of the attempted mugging and how John Oldfield had come to her aid. She thought the alarm showed concern for her, but he interrupted her.

'This John Oldfield, did you tell him about me?'

'Of course not,' she said indignantly, and went on with her story, telling him about where she was staying, about breakfast and exploring the city. But he seemed to have lost interest. His hands had gone to her shoulders, stroking her, and then had encircled her and tried to draw her closer. She struggled, but he grinned down at her.

'There's no need to fight, to pretend you don't want me. This is why you came, isn't it? You are not the first pretty, rich girl who has fallen for a sailor.'

She managed to struggle upright, but he was still holding her.

'Let me go!' she squealed.

'Later. I saw, all the time on the yacht, how you wanted me.'

Romance was forgotten. Carol had never been in a situation remotely like this before, but she had heard other girls talking. Abruptly she brought her knee up, hard, and Juan yelped and let her go. She seized her bag and fled out the door, down the stairs and through the bar before he could move, running up the street as fast as she could.

The blast of a car horn made her stop and turn, and she found herself looking at the taxi that had brought her there, the driver holding the passenger door open.

'Get in!' he instructed, and gratefully she nearly fell into the taxi, which sped away along the narrow street.

'I told you it wasn't the place for you,' the driver said smugly. 'Fortunately I decided to cruise along there just in case you had changed your mind. Where do you want to go now?'

She gave him the address where she was staying and when they got there she tried to give him all the paper money she had with her, but he took only a few notes and then folded the rest and gave them back to her.

'I have a daughter,' he told her, 'and if she needed help I hope someone would give it to her without needing to be paid.'

She waved goodbye to him gratefully and then went up in the lift to her room. She fell on the bed, fully-clothed, and was fast asleep ten minutes after getting out of the taxi.

★   ★   ★

Her mobile phone woke her.

'John Oldfield here,' a voice informed

her briskly. 'I'll pick you up about eight o'clock.'

She mumbled agreement as the phone went dead, and then looked at her watch. Half-past seven! She ran for the bathroom and was standing under the shower before the memory of what had happened earlier that day came back. She shuddered. Freedom was all very well, but on her first day in Barcelona she had nearly been mugged, and on her second day she had fallen foul of Juan! How fortunate that she had John Oldfield to look after her!

Carol showered, rubbed her hair dry, and then put on a t-shirt and skirt and sandals before applying the light touches of make-up that were all her mother approved of. She heard the outside buzzer and the sound of voices, and then there was a knock on her door. When she opened it, John and the señora were both waiting. The little lady eyed her critically from head to foot and then nodded approvingly.

John said something in Spanish, and

the little lady nodded even more vigorously.

'What did you say to her?' Carol asked suspiciously as the ornate lift creaked toward the ground.

'I told her that I thought you looked very charming.'

She was silent, partly because she was unsure how to respond to such a compliment, and partly because she had no idea if that was what he had actually said or not.

Carol was a little daunted by the crowds of people sauntering about the streets as the evening began and took John's arm, taking comfort in having him by her side. He led her towards the heart of the city.

'I know you've probably been here already, but this is the real heart of the city, Las Ramblas,' he remarked, and a few minutes later drew her attention to an iron fountain in the centre of Las Ramblas.

'It is said that if you drink from this fountain you are sure to come back to Barcelona.'

He collected a little water in the palm of his hand and drank it, then looked challengingly at Carol. She followed his example without hesitation, suddenly sure that she would always want to come back to this vibrant city, in spite of what had happened.

They continued their progress. Wide-eyed, Carol was looking everywhere, eager not to miss a thing.

'Instead of walking past everyone, we'll let them walk past us for a while,' John decided after she nearly collided with a lamp post because she had been looking behind her.

He changed direction and took her to a square just off Las Ramblas lined with bars and small restaurants. With a glass of wine and some olives in front of them they watched life pass by.

It would be more accurate to say that Carol watched the passers-by and John watched Carol, amused by her naïve reactions to some of Barcelona's more eccentric inhabitants, and a little concerned by the depression her face revealed when he thought she was not looking.

'What's the matter?' he said finally, when people-watching apparently began to pall and Carol seemed lost in her own thoughts.

She jumped guiltily.

'What do you mean? Nothing's the matter.'

He looked at her steadily, and she could feel herself slowly growing crimson.

'What's the matter? I know something is. I can see it in your face, Carol. Now, what's wrong?'

'Nothing's wrong. I can assure you,' she insisted, and then frowned and shook her head.

'I mean, nothing's the matter now. Something happened earlier, but I dealt with it and it's all over now.'

'No harm done?'

'Only to my pride,' she said bitterly. 'I thought I was being very clever, and instead I was an absolute fool.'

'Well, I've often felt like that,' he said

comfortingly. 'I'm not going to pry any further, so long as you can assure me there won't be any consequences.'

'I can promise you that!' she said with feeling.

Even the idea of seeing Juan again made her feel slightly sick.

'Good. Incidentally, I called your parents and told them that you were now settled in a very respectable establishment and that I was going to keep an eye on you. They were relieved to hear it. I also told them that you had decided to move to a hotel nearer the centre of the city because you felt the one they had chosen was too far from the art galleries and historical monuments which you want to visit.'

He looked at her meaningfully.

'This means that you may have to explain why you have developed a sudden interest in culture, but you won't have to explain that you decided to start a small rebellion against them, unless you want to.'

'So you are going to keep me from

harm,' Carol brooded. 'The adventure seems to have gone, but I'm not going to spend all my time in galleries and museums,' she finished firmly.

3

'Are you ready to go?' he said, looking at his watch. 'I did book a table, and the restaurant may not keep it for us if we're too late.'

The restaurant was only a short walk away and the table had been kept for them. When the waiter left them to make their choice from a long menu Carol looked at John with a crease between her brows.

'Do I choose for myself or do you decide what you think would be best? I don't know half these dishes.'

'Choose what you think you will like, but if you're not certain then I can tell you what's good,' he informed her.

As they waited for the first course he looked at her quizzically.

'Carol, you must have been in a big city before.'

'Only with my parents, and then just

for a day or two, and my mother doesn't like sightseeing.'

She had spent the past few years at boarding school, and told him that several of her holidays had been spent at school because her parents were not at home.

'Didn't your mother think you should be with her during the holidays?'

'Mother said it was her duty to go with my father when he had to travel on business.'

She bit her lip. 'Mother said I would be in the way.'

He put together what she had said with the things he had heard from his own parents, and decided that Mrs Oliver was a woman with little maternal instinct. In spite of the amount of money that had been spent on her care, in some ways Carol had been a neglected child.

'You've been so well brought up that I'm surprised you even thought of rebelling,' he said curiously.

She gave a spontaneous smile which lit up her usually solemn face. 'Perhaps it was television that was to blame. When I was on my own I used to watch quite a lot. I could see that most people led very different lives from mine, and a lot of them seemed to be having fun. I decided I wanted to have some fun.'

'And so you shall, and I will aid and abet you. I can take you out to dinner each night, and I may be able to get away during the day for a few hours, but you will be on your own most of the time, so please listen to some good advice.'

She sat with her hands in her lap, the picture of a good little schoolgirl attending to her teacher.

'First of all,' he began, 'don't talk to strangers. And another thing, where do you keep your emergency money?'

She looked bewildered.

'It's always useful to have a little money hidden away, just in case. My sister, Pat, says she always has a few notes hidden in her pocket, or in a shoe.'

Carol giggled.

'Don't laugh. I have four sisters, remember, and you are getting the benefit of their experience.' He continued giving her what he considered useful tips until the meal ended, when he asked her if she would like to have a coffee in the restaurant or go back to the square.

'I loved the square. Let's go back there.'

As they strolled back to the square she unselfconsciously slipped her arm through his. The last traces of day had long vanished, and the lights in the square showed the cafes and restaurants were full. John finally managed to secure a table and order coffee and Carol sat down with relief.

'I thought we'd never find space! What are all these people doing?'

'Preparing for a night out. Spaniards eat late and play late. A lot of them won't be going home till dawn.'

She sighed with pure happiness. 'I love Barcelona.'

'So do I. I know I'm doing my duty by looking after you, but in fact I'm enjoying this chance to show somebody else how great it is.'

He pulled a small book from his pocket. 'I got you a short guide to the city in English, so you can decide what you want to see.'

She received it with thanks. Leafing through a few more pages of the small book, she looked up to find him regarding her steadily.

'You've changed since we last met several years ago in England. You were round-shouldered and sullen, glaring through your hair at me. I don't think you spoke to me directly once in the whole weekend.'

'Well, you were thin and awkward and kept making silly jokes. Actually, I had braces on my teeth so I hardly spoke to anyone because I didn't want people to see them, but the worst part was that aunt who kept looking at the two of us and saying loudly how wonderful it would be if we got married. It was so embarrassing!'

'I agree,' he said with heart-felt emphasis. 'At least we have both improved considerably since then.'

Carol realised that there was a compliment in this remark, as well as a certain measure of conceit, and a faint blush rose to her face.

'What should I do tomorrow? What are the most important things to see?'

'There are so many! I think the best thing for you to do would be to come to my office after you've had breakfast, and I'll spend the morning showing you the sights.'

The firm of Oliver & Oldfield did not have its own offices in Barcelona, but had an arrangement with a bank which was ready to make an office and secretary available on its premises when required. John gave Carol the details, and then they walked back to the *hostal*.

'Goodnight,' Carol murmured. 'I'm

sorry you've been landed with looking after me.'

'It's been no trouble so far.'

He placed a finger under her chin and tilted her face up to his. 'And whatever happened earlier today, you seem to have coped very well.'

★ ★ ★

It was wonderful to wake up the next morning and realise that a whole day lay ahead in which to explore the city. Juan was fading from her memory remarkably fast, displaced by the charms of Barcelona, and John's parting compliment had boosted her self-confidence.

After having breakfast and leaving the waiter happily counting her tip once more, Carol hailed a taxi and was delivered to a large building near the centre of town. Here she was met by a secretary who informed her that Mr Oldfield would be free soon and would like her to wait in the secretary's office.

Carol sank obediently into a comfortable chair and prepared to wait, as she had often done for her father in the past. After a while she noticed that the busy secretary was occasionally giving her a rather frosty glance and she wondered why. The girl had a pale oval face whose high cheekbones were emphasised by the way her sleek dark hair was drawn back into a bun at the nape of her neck, and she was smartly dressed in a light grey suit with a white blouse.

John Oldfield appeared after a quarter-of-an-hour. His lightweight suit was more formal than last night's sweatshirt and casual trousers and he fitted easily into the businesslike atmosphere.

He greeted Carol, and then turned to the secretary. 'I've left some correspondence to deal with and a few notes on matters that need attention. I'll be back some time this afternoon.'

The girl smiled at him but nodded coolly at Carol as the pair left. In the lift

John pulled off his tie, stuffed it in his pocket and opened the neck of his shirt.

'I can stand the full formal dress thing in an air-conditioned office,' he told Carol, 'but even in June the streets of Barcelona can get too hot for comfort. Now I suggest the first thing we do is have a coffee and discuss matters.'

In five minutes they had reached the central plaza, a large open space where the jetting water from fountains sparkled in the sunlight. John found them a table on the pavement outside a café and ordered coffee.

'Your secretary didn't seem to think much of me,' Carol remarked. 'She gave me some very cold looks.'

'What do you expect? She works very hard for her living and it must be annoying to have some little rich girl wander in with nothing to worry about except how to amuse herself.'

'I don't look like a rich girl. She was looking very smart, and I'm wearing jeans, a t-shirt and a denim jacket.'

'Carol, each of the so-casual pieces of clothing you are wearing has a very expensive designer label.'

'It's not a crime to be rich and I don't need a job.'

'You don't have to have a job, but you could have a purpose in life.'

'I'm only eighteen!'

'Isabella has been working since she was sixteen.'

'What about you? You're rich as well. Why are you in the family firm instead of discovering your purpose in life?'

He looked at her through narrowed eyes, and then shrugged. 'I happen to be very lucky. The family firm helps me fulfil myself. I am really interested in trade, in modern communication. Of course being an Oldfield helped me to get a job which allows me to use my abilities, but the firm doesn't just put up with me because I'm my father's son, I'm a useful member of the team.

'Perhaps I'm just trying to convince myself that I'm good. I know there is always the suspicion among the staff that being an Oldfield has given me an unfair advantage, and that I wouldn't have succeeded quite so easily if I hadn't been my father's son.

'Sometimes I think I should go and work for another firm. If I did well, it would prove to everyone that I've got as far as I have on merit. There would be no more murmurs about nepotism behind my back.'

'And people envy us because we have rich families!' She sighed. 'We're stuck in that together.'

'The Oldfields and Olivers always seem like one big family to me, so I suppose I can regard you as an honorary sister.'

'That's an awful thought!' she said through gritted teeth.

'Well, we seem to be having a typical brother and sister debate, don't we? Except that you don't know what they are like because you are an only child, while I've got four sisters.'

'Could we forget about families and get back to the reason we are here? I want to explore Barcelona, and you're supposed to be helping me do that.'

'True, and today I am spending quite a lot of time with you so that you'll be able to see the best of the city. You're making your bid for freedom in Spain but unfortunately you don't speak the language, which means you had better stick to the tourist trails.'

It seemed a sensible plan, but two hours later Carol was suffering seriously from information overload. She had listened conscientiously to the guidance broadcast on the bus, and had discovered that she had not realised before how varied and extensive were the opportunities that Barcelona offered the tourist.

She and John got off the bus near the top of the hill which overlooked the city, had a light meal at a café, and then from a terrace surrounded by gardens she gazed round at the vista of the city spread before her.

'I've got less than a week to see all

this,' she mourned.

'Go through the guide book and make a list of what you really want to see,' John suggested. 'After all, people come back to Barcelona year after year and find something new each time.'

Carol stifled a yawn and he looked at her. 'I think you are ready for a siesta, and then, dear Miss Oliver,' he said, sweeping her a mock bow, 'perhaps you will do me the honour of letting me take you out for dinner this evening.'

She lifted her chin defiantly. 'If it's a very good meal.'

'You do sound like a sister,' he laughed, then looked round and took her hand. 'Run! There's a bus coming!'

Carol was used to an uneventful quiet life, and so many new experiences had left her exhausted. She was grateful to get back to her small quiet room, tug off her boots and jeans, and fall fast asleep on the bed.

★　★　★

John had decided that the late after-noon and evening were to be devoted to giving Carol an idea of the country around Barcelona, and his powerful little car swooped along cliff-top roads and leafy valleys and carefully navigated its way through busy towns and tiny villages.

They had dinner in one of the resorts. The meal was adequate but undistin-guished, a bland international menu that aimed at offending nobody rather than pleasing a few. Carol could hear other customers speaking English, German, French and even Japanese, but the Span-iards obviously went elsewhere.

John seemed a little preoccupied as well. He apologised when she had to repeat a comment twice.

'Work hasn't been going too smoothly today. I think they were all geared up for your father's arrival, and when I suddenly appeared it threw them a bit, and some of them had left a few things that needed doing to the last minute.'

'So nobody loves you?'

'Nobody ever loves the boss who arrives unexpectedly. Anyway, forget that. Have you had a good day?'

She thought back over the sunlit happy hours, and her lips curved in a contented smile.

'Oh, yes. And the fact that you are busy fits in with my plans for tomorrow. If you don't mind, I want to spend the morning doing things by myself. It isn't just that I can choose what to do and enjoy doing it. I want to be by myself, responsible for myself, with no-one escorting me or keeping a discreet eye on me.'

'Are you saying you don't need my company any more? Your confidence is growing fast,' John said with amusement. 'If the rest of this week is equally successful your parents are going to have trouble with you in the future.'

Her smile became a little defiant. 'I haven't caused them a moment's trouble in eighteen years — apart from that message the other day. Perhaps it's time they had to worry about me a bit.'

'Let's compromise. Spend the morning by yourself, but meet me at the café in the plaza about one o'clock. Then we'll agree what to do next.'

They drove back to Barcelona more slowly, enjoying the warm evening air. With darkness hiding the massed hotels of the resorts, the shimmer of clustered lights had an impressionistic beauty.

The next morning Carol used her guidebook to make her way to an open area called Ciutadella Park, happy to wander through green open spaces again after two days in the centre of the crowded city.

She was an intelligent girl who learned quickly, and John's comments had made her appreciate the fact that designer clothes might indicate a rich target to bag-snatchers or pickpockets. Back in the centre of the city she found a large department store and bought some moderately-priced jeans and tops.

She changed in the toilets, stuffing the designer label garments carelessly into the store's plastic bag, and emerged into the sunshine feeling that she blended a little more easily with all the other tourists.

At half-past twelve she made her way to the café where he had taken her the previous day and settled down there to wait for him with a cup of coffee and a magazine.

A blonde woman in her thirties sat down at the next table, and once or twice when Carol looked up the woman caught her eye and smiled. Perhaps she was travelling on her own and felt lonely and in need of a little conversation, Carol decided.

4

At half-past-one there was still no sign of John. Carol wondered whether to order another cup of coffee. She knew that something unexpected must have made it difficult for John to leave the office, but she hoped he wouldn't be long. She had enjoyed wandering round by herself, but now she wanted to talk to someone about the things she had seen, and John was a pleasant and knowledgeable companion.

There was another reason why Carol wanted John with her. She had discovered that an attractive girl by herself, an obvious tourist, was seen as fair game by some men who tried to persuade her that she needed their company and guidance around the city.

Even now, sitting by herself at a café table, she was attracting admiring glances. Two young men in turn asked hopefully if they could share her table, but a firm shake of the head was enough to send them away. Then another man appeared who was unpleasantly persistent and she deliberately turned her back on him.

To her horror, in spite of her obvious rejection of his advances, he pulled out a chair and sat himself beside her at the table. Carol had never had to deal with behaviour like this before and felt a little panicky.

Not knowing what to do, she looked around anxiously, hoping to see John. Instead she found that the blonde woman not only smiled sympathetically, she offered Carol help.

'Why don't you come and join me?' she suggested in English. 'Then that unpleasant young man will be left by himself.'

Gladly Carol picked up her cup and moved to the woman's table. 'Thank you,' she said with a nervous smile.

The woman laughed. 'I've obviously had more practice than you at dealing with pests,' she said in a voice loud enough to be heard by the man, who looked angry at being so pointedly abandoned, fidgeted uneasily for a while, and then stood up and walked away much to Carol's relief.

'I'm Anna Dreiser, by the way,' the woman said. Her English was excellent, with a slight accent which Carol could not place immediately.

'I'm Carol — Carol Oliver — and I'm very grateful for your help.'

'Women on their own should help each other,' Anna Dreiser observed.

'Oh, I'm not on my own. I'm waiting for a friend,' she frowned at her watch. 'But he's very late now.'

'Well, let me order us both another coffee while you wait and we can get to know each other till he arrives. I don't think anyone will dare approach the two of us.'

In the next few minutes Carol learned that Anna Dreiser was from Switzerland, and that she was accompanying her husband on a business trip but was spending a few days by herself in Barcelona.

'I don't find visiting factories very interesting,' she said wryly, and then looked expectantly at Carol.

'I'm here by myself till the end of the week,' Carol said a little awkwardly. She did not want to tell this stranger the whole complicated story. 'My parents are joining me then.'

'This friend you are waiting for? Is he just a friend or is he a boyfriend?'

'Just a friend,' Carol said hurriedly. 'In fact, he's a family friend who's been asked to keep an eye on me.'

'He doesn't seem to be doing a very good job today. When was he supposed to meet you?'

'One o' clock.'

'It's after two o'clock now. Are you sure he's coming?'

'Something must have cropped up to stop him getting away,' Carol said slowly. If that was what had happened, John should have been able to call her. She supposed she could telephone his office, but if she did that she would only be able to reach him through the disapproving Isabella. Perhaps she should try to find out what had happened, though.

Anna Dreiser interrupted her thoughts. 'What were you planning to do this afternoon?'

'We were going to Guëll Park. Apparently there is some amazing architecture there.'

'That is a coincidence! I was planning to do the same thing! Why don't we get together? After all, your family friend can't expect you to wait here for him all afternoon, and if he does get away later presumably he will go straight to the Park.'

'I don't know,' Carol said uneasily. John's warnings about talking to strangers were coming back to her and she was sure that he would strongly disapprove if she went off with someone she had only met a few minutes ago.

Her companion shrugged. 'Oh, well,

if you want to hang around here being pestered . . . '

Carol felt that she was somehow being rude by rejecting the woman's kind offer to take her with her, that the woman was hurt by her hesitation.

'I suppose I've waited long enough, but I would like to call him.'

'I'm sure he won't expect you to be here still,' Anna Dreiser said firmly, 'but it might be a mistake to call him. If he is in an important meeting he won't want to be interrupted.'

Carol hadn't thought of that, but now she remembered how often her mother had emphasised that she would never disturb her husband at work except for a dire emergency.

'I told my chauffeur to be here for two o'clock,' Anna Dreiser said a little impatiently. 'You can always use my car phone if you want to.'

This made up Carol's mind for her. She was used to a world where wives filled in the hours being driven in chauffeur-driven limousines while their husbands were occupied with business matters. She felt her family would have approved of Anna Dreiser. 'I would like to come with you,' she said a little shyly.

Anna slid some currency under her coffee cup and stood up decisively. 'Excellent! We can keep each other company for the afternoon and your friend won't have to worry about you.'

Carol was aware of niggling doubts as her new friend led the way. Suppose John was already on his way here? Did she really want to tour Barcelona with this stranger? She was so much older than herself that it would be like going out with her mother.

She hesitated and her steps slowed, but at that moment the woman turned and beckoned impatiently. 'My car is here waiting!'

It was difficult for Carol to see how she was going to get out of the situation now. However, the sight of Anna Dreiser's car, parked in a side street, reassured her. It was large, black, sleek and expensive. Nobody with a car like that could be plotting any minor misdemeanour.

The chauffeur was dressed in black and even wore the traditional peaked cap. As he saw his mistress approach he slid smoothly out of the driving seat and opened the passenger door. The engine was already running as Anna Dreiser got in and the chauffeur waited, holding the door open for Carol. She glanced at him and nodded her thanks shyly, but the peak of his cap hid his face.

Just as she was going to bend her head and get in the car, to her relief she saw a familiar figure striding hastily along the street. Her face lit up, and she waved vigorously.

'John's here at last!' she exclaimed. 'Thank you for your offer, but I won't need a lift after all,' but as she turned to go towards John she found the chauffeur was standing holding the door in such a way that she could not move.

'Excuse me,' she said, pointing to John. 'I want to go there.'

Instead of moving, the chauffeur unexpectedly gave her a violent shove that forced her into the interior of the car. Anna Dreiser's arms went round her, preventing her escape, and one hand went over Carol's mouth before she could scream for help.

John had seen her now and seen what was happening and was racing towards the black car, coming to her rescue for a second time. The chauffeur stepped back, as if reluctant to face a very angry young man, and John pushed past him and leant into the back of the car, stretching out his hands to Carol. 'Quick! Come with me!'

As she gladly stretched out her arms towards him, though, two things happened. Carol felt a sharp prick like a large needle in her back, and the chauffeur produced an ugly little blackjack which he swung hard against the back of John's head. As Carol felt her head begin to whirl she was aware of the chauffeur bundling John into the car and slamming the door.

The street had not been completely empty and a couple of passers-by saw the little scuffle and started to move towards the car. But the powerful engine was already roaring into action and the car took off at speed, its tyres squealing. The pursuers stopped, looked at each other, and shrugged. Could they be sure exactly what they had seen in those few crowded seconds? Did they want to get mixed up with the police on such vague grounds? They decided not.

The car did not stop till it reached a side road outside Barcelona, where it drove into a scrap yard, coming to a halt near a small dirty white van. Two men climbed out of the van and came over to the car, where Anna Dreiser and the chauffeur got out to meet them.

'Is this the girl?' Anna Dreiser asked, indicating the unconscious Carol.

Juan Sastre peered into the car and nodded vigorously. 'That's her, that's the Oliver heiress. I told you her family will pay a lot for her.'

The woman looked at John with cold calculation. 'She said he was a friend. He's no use to us. We'll get rid of him.'

'No!' Juan interrupted. 'He's probably John Oldfield, son of her father's partner. The girl said he had come to Barcelona to look after her.'

Anna Dreiser laughed triumphantly. 'Two birds with one stone! We can ask for twice as much ransom.'

Juan grinned. 'You wouldn't have known if I hadn't told you. Doesn't that mean that I should get paid twice as much?'

'Oh, you'll get your full reward,' Anna Dreiser told him, smiling. She nodded to the other man who had been in the van with Juan. There was a swift movement and the knife in his back meant that Juan Sastre was dead before his body hit the ground.

'Move these two to the van,' ordered Anna Dreiser.

★ ★ ★

By the time the police searched that area the following day the big black car was a burnt-out wreck and Juan's body was hidden in a rough grave in the woods.

Carol was shaken into awareness when her head hit something hard. Groggily she tried to make out where she was and discovered that she was sliding helplessly about on a surface of ridged metal with sufficient force to bruise herself as she hit the sides.

The constant roar of an engine made her head hurt even more, but the most frightening thing about her situation was the complete and utter darkness that surrounded her.

Then, as she scrabbled to sit up, one foot caught on something soft and warm and she heard a groan. She froze, her heart beating wildly.

As she heard another groan she gradually recalled her last moments of consciousness as she fought against the drug Anna Dreiser had injected, and the memory came back to John's body sprawled on the floor of the car, the last thing she saw before she sank into oblivion.

'John?' she tried to say, but her dry mouth could scarcely form the word. She swallowed and tried again. 'John?'

There was a sigh, then silence. Desperately, Carol managed to get to her knees and feel for the inert body. Her questing hands found an arm and she felt along it towards the head with vague ideas of checking for injuries. Her hand reached the face and was pushed aside.

'Take your finger out of my eye!' commanded a weak voice, and she could have sobbed with relief to hear his voice.

'How are you?' she said anxiously.

There was silence, and then the sound of movement. 'As far as I can tell, I'm all right except for a really awful headache.' His voice changed. 'And I feel sick.'

'Don't,' she said pleadingly, and after a few seconds there was a shuffling movement and an uncertain laugh.

'No need to panic. I feel better sitting upright. How are you?'

'Thirsty and a bit bruised,' she admitted.

'What happened? I saw you in a car with some woman and she seemed to be holding you back. Then somebody hit me.'

'A man was pestering me and so this woman invited me to sit with her . . . '

Carol poured out an explanation of what had happened, and there was another silence, broken by an exasperated exclamation. 'I thought I told you not to speak to strangers!'

'But she looked so respectable!' she said defensively.

'Did you expect her to wear a label saying 'kidnapper'?'

In the darkness Carol's eyes widened in horror. 'Do you think that is what she is?'

'What else? She abducted you pretty smoothly, and thanks to my timely arrival she's now got two hostages instead of one.'

'I'm sorry.' Carol's voice broke suddenly and she burst into tears.

She heard John moving, and then his arm fumbled its way round her shoulders and some soft fabric was thrust into her hand.

'Here! At least I've got a handkerchief to offer a lady.'

She took the handkerchief gratefully and felt his hand patting her shoulder. 'It's too late to start fretting about what has happened. We've got to decide what to do now.'

Her sobs gradually stopped and she blew her nose loudly on his handkerchief. 'What can we do?'

'Evaluate the situation.' He spoke briskly, trying to conceal from her his own apprehensions. Whoever had taken them captive had been efficient, ruthless and brutal. What lay ahead could be very unpleasant.

'In the first place, this obviously wasn't a spur of the moment job. The woman had the car waiting and a hypodermic ready to drug you. We have obviously been transferred from the car to a van. That means there must be at least one other person involved as well as the woman and the chauffeur. It looks like a well-organised gang at work.'

He felt her shiver and gave her another comforting pat. 'That could be a good thing. If they are professional criminals then they just want to get their money and make their escape. They'll have planned ahead and won't panic or do anything stupid.'

He hurried on before she could consider what he might mean by 'anything stupid'. 'They'll take reasonable care of us and get matters moving as quickly as they can. It's possible that they have already sent ransom demands to our parents.'

'How much do you think they'll ask?'

'They'll have read the company accounts and know how well it is doing. For the only Oliver child and the eldest Oldfield son I expect they will ask a lot.'

He mentioned a sum that made her gasp.

'Can our parents pay that much quickly?'

'The banks will help.'

The banks might also see it as an opportunity to demand a share of the firm in return, he thought bitterly.

Carol was reacting from her former despair with something approaching anger. 'Are we just going to let them treat us as objects, like a pair of parcels? Can't we try to escape?'

At this moment the vehicle must have turned a sharp corner, for they were thrown across the van floor. Seconds later it happened again.

'As far as I can tell,' John said, 'we are being driven up a steep road and the van hasn't had to stop for any traffic lights or crossroads, and I haven't heard any other vehicles pass it. I think we are being taken somewhere in the hills not far from Barcelona. I don't know how long we've been travelling, however, because they must have drugged me as well. The blow on the head wouldn't have kept me unconscious for long.'

'So just screaming isn't going to do any good because there won't be anybody within earshot who might help us,' Carol deduced gloomily.

'If only we could get away from them, even for just a short time, the forests are so thick on these hills that they might not be able to follow us,' John said slowly. 'If we are still apparently half-unconscious when they open the van doors to get us out, it might make them careless. Once we are out of the van we could make a run for it, but it's a slim chance.'

'It's better than being treated like an object,' Carol said fiercely. 'I'm willing to try it.'

'If there is an opportunity, if we are both out of the van and not being held, then we'll run, but we've got to keep together.' The van lurched again and they clung to each other, both trying to conceal their own fear for the sake of the other.

Eventually the van did come to a halt. There was an interval during which John and Carol hastily lay down and closed their eyes, then the sound of footsteps approaching the van doors and the grating of the key being turned in a lock. Suddenly the bright Spanish sun slanted into the van's interior.

'Out!' came the command, and the prone figures were shaken unceremoniously. John and Carol sat up with apparent difficulty and reluctance and stared up at the man who was looking in at them. He was about thirty, very dark and swarthy, with thick black hair and eyebrows, dressed in jeans and a black sweatshirt. With a shock Carol recognised him at once.

'That's the man who was pestering me at the café!' she told John.

'And so forcing you to take shelter with me,' Anna Dreiser said crisply as she came into sight and stood by her accomplice. 'Now, get out of here. I haven't time to hang about.'

Slowly exaggerating their stiffness, John and Carol climbed down from the van and found themselves standing on a steep narrow road with woods all around. Near the van a building was just visible over a high wall. The man pushed a door in the wall open just wide enough for one person to enter and Anna Dreiser pointed to the gap. 'In there,' she ordered.

Carol looked at John and saw his jaw tighten. Once inside that gate they would be imprisoned. Their only chance of a break for freedom was now.

'Run!' John shouted fiercely, grabbing Carol's hand, and the two of them suddenly leapt into action, racing down the road towards the first bend and leaving their kidnappers standing momentarily amazed and motionless.

Within a few strides Carol's legs felt weak and rubbery. After being drugged and shaken about in the van she had great difficulty controlling her limbs and felt near to collapse, but she forced herself on. It was her fault they were in this mess and she couldn't fail now. If they could hide themselves among the trees they might yet escape.

'Into the woods when we get round the bend!' panted John, but as he spoke there was a sudden crack and a vicious hum. A twig was torn off a bush inches from them and a grey splash appeared on a rock ahead. John halted so abruptly that Carol, continuing to run, lost her footing and fell, pulling him down beside her.

'What's the matter? Why did you stop like that?' she demanded.

His face was white and set. 'We can't outrun a bullet.'

The woman strode towards them, a pistol held in her right hand. 'Very sensible, Mr Oldfield,' she said coldly. 'Now do as you are told.'

Crestfallen, the two climbed to their feet and slowly trudged back to the gate and this time they went through it obediently into captivity. They found themselves in an enclosure containing a dilapidated one-storey dwelling built into a corner of the high wall which enclosed the building and a neglected yard. The building had a terrace on two sides, shaded by neglected vines growing on a rough trellis.

Anna Dreiser gestured sharply to the man, who went into the building. 'Apart from that amateurish attempt to escape, I am glad to see that you are both sensible people,' she told her captives. 'At least, you haven't started blustering and telling me I can't do what I have clearly already done. As you have no doubt realised, this is a kidnapping. We are interested in you only as a means of obtaining money.

'We had planned to take you alone, Miss Oliver, but Mr Oldfield is undoubtedly a bonus and I look forward to increasing our profit considerably. Soon I shall start negotiations, and your futures will be much brighter if everything goes smoothly. We don't want the bother of looking after you for too long.

'Let me explain what happens to you now. This hut belongs to an acquaintance of mine. It is in a lonely part of the hills and is only used during the hunting season. There are two rooms. You will have one and Sanchez will occupy the other. Please note that there is new razor wire all round the wall and the gate, and there are other security measures. Sanchez!'

As she raised her voice her accomplice reappeared. Now he was carrying a shotgun in one hand and grasping a dog's lead in the other. The dog was big, gaunt, and unkempt, snarling and struggling as it fought to escape. Carol shrank back in very real fear.

'If you try to escape, Sanchez will shoot and the dog will attack you. If by some miracle you did get outside this yard, you would find yourselves in a wilderness miles from anywhere, and the dog would soon track you down, so I suggest you resign yourself to staying here. If you do as you are told life will be bearable, if not enjoyable. If you don't, it will be very unpleasant, and could unfortunately be cut short.'

They stood silent and depressed before her. She looked at them contemptuously. 'Well, just one more thing to do and then I'll leave you to Sanchez.'

She took a mobile telephone from her pocket and rapidly keyed in a number. Apparently there was a rapid reply, for she nodded in satisfaction before she spoke.

'Miss Isabella Sanchez? Listen carefully. I have kidnapped Miss Carol Oliver and Mr John Oldfield and will hold them prisoner until I have received the ransom I require. I will call again in an hour or so to give further details, and I will expect to speak to Mr Oliver or Mr Oldfield, no-one else. I will now give you proof that I have indeed kidnapped the couple.'

She beckoned John closer and held out the telephone. 'Speak to her,' she ordered curtly.

John bent close to the little instrument. 'Isabella! We are at . . . '

Before he could say another word Sanchez had knocked him away roughly and Anna Dreiser cut the connection.

'Good try,' she said coolly. 'Thank you for that. I think the girl will be convinced that you are indeed in trouble.' She slipped the phone back into her pocket, nodded to Sanchez, and went out through the gate, which Sanchez padlocked behind her, putting the key in his pocket. They heard the van start up and drive away.

In Barcelona, Isabella Sanchez was already frantically dialling the emergency number that would put her in contact with the Olivers and the Oldfields.

5

John and Carol stood waiting nervously to see what happened next, but Sanchez ignored them as he chained the dog to a wooden post, picked up the shotgun and disappeared through one of the two doors that opened on to the terrace. Presumably it led to his quarters. When he had disappeared John walked across the yard and stared up at the razor wire which made such a terrifying barrier around it. At once the dog started to bark furiously, straining at the chain which kept him from attacking John. Sanchez instantly appeared with his gun at the ready and gestured John back towards the house.

'Let's see what has been prepared for us,' John remarked resignedly and led Carol through the other door. They found themselves in a windowless room, dimly lit by the light from the doorway. Carol stood in the middle and looked round unbelievingly.

'Is this all?' she said.

It was not an attractive place. The roof was made of crude planks; the walls had been whitewashed a long time ago and were now stained with damp, and green with moss in places. The floor was covered with cracked and uneven tiles and here and there a straggly plant was pushing its way up between them. A door, which must once have opened into Sanchez's room, had been roughly bricked up. The furniture consisted of a small table with two chairs and a camp bed covered with some old blankets. There was nothing else in the room.

'They're certainly not taking any chances of us using something as a weapon or a means to escape,' John observed.

He patted his pockets. 'Someone's already taken anything that might be useful. I did have a penknife and a book of matches, but all they've left me is one handkerchief and a hundred Euros. Oh, and a small comb. At least we will be able to keep our hair tidy.' He looked at his wrist and then at Carol's. 'Even our watches are gone. Definitely professionals.'

There was a hint of reluctant admiration in his voice as he acknowledged the kidnappers' efficiency.

'Are we supposed to spend all our time in here?' Carol said plaintively.

'I hope not. I'm going to see if we are allowed out on the terrace at least.'

Trying to look unconcerned, he strolled out into the sunlight and walked along the terrace. While he stayed on the terrace nothing happened. The dog's lips peeled back from its big yellow teeth but it remained silent. However as soon as John ventured off the terrace the animal stood up, bristling, only subsiding when John went back near the house.

'At least we don't have to stay indoors,' he reported. 'We can go out on the terrace, but no further apparently, and the dog will warn Sanchez if we try anything.'

Carol was looking uncomfortable and shifted uneasily. 'What about a bathroom?'

John sighed. 'You don't get bathrooms in abandoned huts, Carol. However, if you go outside you'll see a kind of sentry box attached to the wall. Next to it you'll see a tap. I'm afraid that is all there is here in the way of conveniences.'

She went to check on what he said and came back looking appalled. 'I can't live like this!'

'Millions do,' he pointed out hardheartedly, afraid that sympathy might produce more tears.

For a moment her lip did quiver uncertainly, and then she forced a smile. 'To think I was bored with luxury hotels!'

Unexpectedly they found themselves laughing. It was hysteria rather than mirth, and it didn't last long, but it was oddly comforting. Carol found herself thinking how fortunate she was to have

John with her in this awful situation, as she imagined how scared and lonely she would have been by herself.

'Well, it looks as if life is going to be very basic for the next few days,' John said briskly. 'May I suggest that we move the table and chairs out on the terrace so that we can relax in the fresh air?'

Carol eyed the dog warily as they did this, but apart from watching their every move he showed no hostility. They sat in silence, deep in their individual thoughts. Carol thought of her parents and wondered whether they had been contacted yet and what their reaction would be.

She could imagine her superbly-efficient father coolly considering what should be done and then going into action, but she was unsure how her mother would behave. Would she become hysterical with fear for her only child, or would she be annoyed that Carol had disturbed her busy lifestyle? What could the two fathers do except obey instructions from Anna Dreiser? She looked at John.

'Do you think our parents will go to the police?'

He tilted the crude wooden chair back. 'I was wondering about that. I assume they will be told not to contact the authorities, but I expect they will anyway. Kidnapping has become a serious problem in some countries and the police forces have special squads to deal with it.'

'How long do you think we will be here?'

He pursed his lips, considering. 'Four or five days at least. It will take time to assemble the kind of money that will be demanded as ransom.'

'Can't the police get the kidnappers when they go to collect the ransom?'

'They won't be collecting cash from a waste bin, Carol. As I said, this gang is very efficient. Money can be transferred round the world electronically very rapidly. If it were to be transferred through a few off-shore accounts it would be very difficult to trace before it was turned into cash or bearer bonds.'

For a moment she was a spoiled child again. 'Can't you do anything instead of just sitting there?' she snapped.

He turned to her impatiently. 'Can you suggest anything? I'm a business-man, not some superhero!'

She was about to make some retort, then stayed silent as she saw him clearly. Here was a young man desper-ately worried for her as well as himself, and she must not make matters worse.

'What I would like to know,' he brooded, 'was how the gang knew who you were and how to find you. After all, heiresses don't go wandering around the city streets very often. I was coming round a bit when they transferred us from the car to the van and I heard some Spaniard identify you as Carol Oliver. Who knew you in Barcelona?'

Carol closed her eyes in horror. When she opened them, John was staring at her. 'It must have been Juan!' she said unbelievingly.

'Who?'

'Juan Sanchez. My parents were right. I did come to Barcelona to meet a man, but you found me before I had contacted him.' Miserably she told him the sorry story of her attraction to Juan, and the meeting in the sordid bar. When she had finished, John groaned and clutched his head.

He looked at her in disgust. 'I should have known it was infatuation and not a desire for liberty.'

Carol's cheeks were flaming. 'It was — partly. And I did realise how horrible he was!'

John sighed explosively. 'Oh well, there's no point in brooding on how we got here. It's what happens now that is important.'

He looked at her drooping, disconsolate figure and stretched out a comforting hand. 'I've done some pretty stupid things in my time, and I've been lucky to avoid disaster. Remind me to tell you about the dark-haired lady who stole my wallet some time.'

She grasped his hand. 'I suppose there are a good few people who would be quite amused to see us here,' he went on. 'The hopes of the Olivers and the Oldfields held prisoner in a hut. They'd feel we were finally getting a dose of reality.'

'Luxury hotels and comfortable bathrooms are real as well,' she said wistfully.

The sun moved towards the horizon. It seemed impossible that in a few hours she had been snatched from freedom in Barcelona to this prison. Twenty-four hours ago she had been sitting with a glass of wine watching the world go by. Now the world had shrunk to this walled enclosure.

Suddenly a door opened and Sanchez appeared, shotgun in one hand and a dish in the other. Approaching them, he slapped the dish on the table. To Carol's surprise, John smiled at the surly Spaniard and thanked him, though he got no response before Sanchez retreated to his own room.

'Why be nice to that awful man?' she said furiously.

'Haven't you read anything about kidnappings? The first thing to do is to try and get on friendly terms with the people holding you hostage. At the least, they will be reluctant to harm you, and with luck they might be persuaded to help you.'

'I don't think you'll have much luck with him,' she observed before turning her horrified attention to their meal.

On the battered tin plate was a hunk of bread, some cold baked beans and slices of tinned meat. Carol viewed it with disgust. 'I can't eat that!' she said, pushing the plate away.

John was already dividing up the bread, using his share to scoop up the beans. 'How long can you go without food? I said four or five days, but it could be much longer. You'd better eat it, because I don't think we'll get anything better. Just be glad we are getting this.'

Reluctantly she started to eat. She

had only had a cup of coffee since breakfast and once she had begun to eat hunger made the food palatable. Looking across, she saw that John had left a slice of meat out of his share.

'Don't you want that? I'll have it then.'

He grinned. 'I thought you couldn't eat it! However, I'm keeping it to try an experiment. Sanchez may not succumb to my approaches, but we'll see about the dog.'

Checking that Sanchez was still out of sight, he tossed half the segment of meat near the dog, who pounced on it and devoured it instantly, then looked hopefully at John, only to sink back into lethargy when he saw no more food was coming his way. John hid the rest of the meat in his pocket and looked at the plate, now cleared of all food.

'Attention to detail again. No knife or fork, because they could be used as weapons, and the plate is made of very soft metal. No glass or pottery, because we could break that into sharp pieces. I wonder how many times Madam Dreiser and her accomplices have done this, and where she comes from. She spoke to us in English, and did you notice that she spoke to Isabella Sanchez in English when you might have expected her to use Spanish? Maybe she comes from some country where Spanish is not very widely known, or maybe she just wanted to be sure that you would understand her.'

Gradually as they sat there, the sky darkened and mosquitoes were whining around them, but they were reluctant to go in the dark, stuffy room. At about nine o'clock Sanchez reappeared and indicated that they should go inside. They seemed to move too slowly for him, for as they got reluctantly to their feet he untied the dog, who stood up, shook himself, and then snarled. Hurriedly Carol and John took refuge in their room.

They stood in the gloom looking at the sparse furniture. With no window or artificial light, there was obviously nothing to do but try to sleep, and in fact both of them felt in need of rest.

'I'll be a gentleman, of course, and let you have the bed, but can you spare me a blanket?' John asked.

Carol lay down on the canvas bed and John rolled himself in his blanket on the floor.

Neither expected to sleep, but both lay still, listening to the other's breathing, until Carol whispered, 'John!'

He sat up. 'What's the matter?'

'When you said we were lucky to get that awful food, what did you mean?'

He did not reply at first, then said reluctantly, 'You eat to live. Feeding us means that they intend to keep us alive.'

He heard her sit up. 'But surely they've got to keep us alive! When they've got the ransom they'll have to let us go.' Her voice tailed off.

'Carol,' John said bleakly, 'they've made no attempt to hide their faces from us. That telephone call to Isabella proved that they are holding us and I expect the ransom is being assembled even now. We have served our purpose. I suspect that they are keeping us alive just in case of some crisis, but I don't believe they intend to set us free. If we are going to do anything, we'll have to do it tomorrow.'

He heard a sob. 'John, I'm f-frightened,' Carol stammered.

He rose swiftly and went to the narrow bed, taking her in his arms. She was shuddering with fear and he held her close, murmuring soothingly, until she was still. Then he lay down with her and they spent the rest of the night holding each other for comfort.

Carol woke first and could see sunlight shining through the gaps in the ill-fitting door. John was snoring gently as she slipped out to the 'sentry box'. The dog, still wandering the yard, barked loudly but made no attempt to approach her, and Sanchez soon appeared and chained the dog up. Carol returned to their room to find John sitting up and yawning.

'Good morning,' she greeted him,

'though I'm not sure what time it is.'

John stood, stretched, and went out, announcing on his return that he thought it was probably about seven o'clock.

'How do you feel?' he asked.

'Dirty!' she said passionately. 'I've been wearing these clothes for twenty-four hours, and I haven't washed or cleaned my teeth since I put them on.'

'At least we have a tap,' he said philosophically, stripping off his shirt. She followed him and watched as he splashed and shivered under the cold water and then tried to dab himself dry with his handkerchief. She washed her face and arms after he had finished and then turned to him.

'What do we do now?'

'We wait, and try to think of a good idea,' he said resignedly.

So they sat down on the terrace and waited. Carol was wistfully recalling breakfasts of hot fresh coffee and croissants, but had to be satisfied with water from the tap and some dry bread, which Sanchez finally brought.

'Nothing for the dog this time,' Carol said, chasing the last few crumbs.

The hours passed very slowly. The wall round the enclosure was so high that all they could see were the tops of trees. The flight of a bird was followed with interest, and ants scurrying away with a crumb of bread were watched with fascination.

'I'd pay a great deal for a notebook and a pencil,' John sighed. 'I could work out business plans, write my memoirs, play noughts and crosses with you.'

'Don't get your hopes up. Our families and the authorities don't know if we are in these forests or in some cellar in Barcelona, or even in some ship on the Mediterranean.'

'Then what can we do?'

'We may have one chance.'

6

John refused to tell Carol what he was thinking of. 'It's an outside chance and I'm hoping to think of something better,' was all he would say.

'But if it doesn't work?'

'If it doesn't, it just means that we die a little sooner.'

'All right — but when will you tell me?'

'Later, when both Sanchez and the dog think we are settling down for the night.'

So once again there was nothing to do but sit and wait. Carol knew without question what she wanted most of all in the world — a luxurious bathroom where she could have a long, hot bath with plenty of bubbles, soft warm towels to dry herself, and then a cup of good coffee. Meanwhile she would have been very grateful for some cream to soothe the mosquito bites that plagued both of them.

She and John whiled away some of the tedious hours by dreaming up elaborate menus for the meals they would enjoy when they reached freedom. At other times they talked about their very different families.

'I always envied you for the way your family seemed so close and happy, yet gave you your freedom when you wanted it,' Carol said wistfully.

John looked thoughtful. 'It was great for most of the time,' he agreed, 'but I didn't have to ask for my freedom. Sometimes it felt as if I was being pushed out of the nest too soon, that I was being tested before I was ready.'

'But it showed your father had confidence in you!'

'Yes.' There was a pause. 'Unfailing confidence. The trouble was that I never dared admit when I was scared or not sure that I could cope. I could never go to my father and admit failure because he took it for granted that I would always succeed. It was a very lonely feeling sometimes. I think that may be the reason I decided to join the family firm. Secretly I thought that if I did do something wrong I would be given just that little extra leeway because I was the son of one of the big bosses. Well, in the future I'm going to test myself without the family safety net.'

'You have succeeded, so your father's judgment was right. And you always look so confident.'

'I've made my share of mistakes, though fortunately so far I have been able to put things right. The air of confidence has sometimes been a bluff.'

'I've had the opposite problem, of course. My father desperately wanted a son to succeed him, and all he got was one not very bright little girl. My mother is a marvellous wife, but I think motherhood bores her. It might have been different if I'd been beautiful like her. She could have been proud of me, shown me off to her friends, but then I turned out to be a plain little thing, so I've never been very close to either of my parents. They never expected anything from me, so I haven't done or achieved anything.'

'Don't think so little of yourself,' he said warmly. 'You are bright, and you are also brave. With a lot of girls I've known I would have been coping with non-stop hysterics from the moment we got here. And you may have been a plain little thing once, but you are definitely improving.'

She laughed, her face lighting up for a few seconds, and John decided that though she was not a classical beauty she was indeed attractive, with a character that was likely to prove a more lasting quality than a pretty face.

'Here comes our host, and I'm afraid we are going to bed supperless,' John warned her, composing his face into a welcoming smile. Sanchez, who had spent the afternoon in his own room, looked at them with an expression that came close to contempt, leant heavily on the table and motioned them to go inside.

Carol noticed that as the man bent over the table, John suddenly lifted his head alertly, as though something had attracted his attention.

'What's the matter?' she enquired when Sanchez had left.

John took her hand as they went into the little room and led her to sit beside him on the camp bed. 'We're going to escape tonight,' he said flatly.

'What?'

He turned on her almost angrily. 'Keep quiet and listen!' he said in a furious whisper. 'I think we've finally found Sanchez's weakness. Tonight I could smell brandy on his breath. He must be even more bored than we are and it seems that he is comforting himself with a bottle, so he's going to be a little less ready to leap into action if he hears a noise, and hopefully a little less accurate with the shotgun.'

She shook her head in confusion. 'What are you proposing to do exactly?

How can we get over the wall?'

He patted the bed. 'The wall is about eight feet high, and I propose to throw these blankets over the razor wire, pull myself up and then pull you up after me. Then we run. Nice and simple.'

'Aren't you forgetting the dog?'

He sighed heavily. 'That's the unknown element. I hope we can distract it for a few vital seconds.'

She was silent for some time, twisting her hands together, and he grew anxious. 'Can you think of anything better?'

'I think the risk is too great. The probability is that we'll either be shot by Sanchez or savaged by the dog. I think it would be safer to just wait for a few days to see if we're released when the kidnappers get the ransom. I can't believe they will kill us in cold blood.'

He shifted restlessly on the narrow bed. 'Carol, everything that has happened has shown that this gang are professionals who have considered every detail. If we are released we can give them a full description of Sanchez, details of the van that brought us here including its number, the rough location of this place, and, most importantly, a full description of Anna Dreiser, who is evidently one of the leaders. They won't want us passing on that information to the authorities.'

Carol began to shiver, and he put his arm round her, but this time even the warm contact with him could not comfort her. 'They want us alive a little while longer, just in case our families demand proof that we haven't been killed, and if something went wrong they could bargain our safety for their freedom, but every hour that passes means that they are nearer to success. I expect Sanchez has a mobile phone. All they've got to do is call him and say they have the money, and he won't hesitate to get rid of us.'

He hugged her closer. 'Come on, Carol. We've got to try to escape, and tonight may be our only chance. If we do fail, probably we'll just end up back in this hut with a few scratches and a furious Sanchez.'

Gradually she stopped shivering and sat up. If there was the slightest chance to get away they had to take it, of course. 'You'll look a fool if Sanchez just had one small drink and the dog decides to eat you,' she said tartly, and he laughed with relief.

'I take it that means you are willing to try to escape. We'd better wait for an hour to make sure that Sanchez is asleep, drunk or sober.'

That hour seemed to stretch out endlessly, except when Carol thought of the moments when she and John would have to go into action. Then time seemed to be passing with unnatural rapidity. The two said little to each other, occupied with their own thoughts and fears.

Finally John stirred. 'It's now or never. Shall we go?'

Carol stood up on legs that had gone strangely weak. 'I'm ready.'

He was gathering up the blankets.

'I'll go out first and try and distract the dog. If that works we make for the wall and I'll throw the blankets over the wire and pull myself up. Then I'll reach down and pull you up. Once we are over the wall we need to get away as far as possible as quickly as possible, so we'll go down the track at first.'

He made it all sound very simple, she thought. 'John,' she said carefully, 'I'm sorry I got us into this mess, and thank you for trying to rescue me from my foolishness, whatever happens next.'

He bent and kissed her lightly on the cheek. 'I always wanted to be a knight errant.'

He opened the door with infinite care. 'There's plenty of moonlight so we can see what we're doing. Let's hope Sanchez is too drunk to see straight. Now, watch how the dog reacts and then follow me to the wall.'

He stepped on to the terrace and walked out into the yard without hesitating. The dog had been snuffling in a corner, but instantly lifted its head alertly and looked at him, made an uncertain movement and then stopped.

Still walking, John tossed the small piece of rancid meat he had saved from the previous day on to the ground a few feet from the animal. There was a scrabble of paws as the hungry dog made for the meat and gulped it down, and in those seconds John reached the wall and tossed the thin blankets up to cover the glittering deadly razor wire that crowned it. Carol was close behind him.

The dog raised its head from its search for more meat, snarled and began to move towards her. John leapt up, grasped the top of the wall and pulled himself up, and then swung round and reached down to where Carol was stretching her hands towards his.

At this moment the dog started barking urgently. The sound made them freeze momentarily, then John was whispering urgently to Carol, 'Hurry! Try to walk up the wall when I'm pulling you up.'

Now the dog, still barking, ran towards them, but John had Carol's hands in a firm grasp and was pulling hard.

Just as she straddled the top of the wall the dog started leaping up, trying to reach them. At the same time they heard Sanchez's door open and as they fell to the ground together on the far side of the wall they heard a roar of anger, the blast of the shotgun, and an agonised yelp from the dog.

They were both up and running down the moonlit path, their hearts thumping. They passed the point where Anna Dreiser's pistol had ended that first futile escape attempt and ran on, not daring to look back to see if Sanchez was pursuing them. John took Carol's hand and pulled her off the path and into the forest.

It was desperately hard going as they blundered about in the dark. Tree branches grew low as they had to bend to make any progress, and the thick undergrowth caught at their feet. After a while Carol sank to the ground. 'I need a rest — just a minute or two.'

John collapsed beside her. 'I feel the same.' As she stopped panting and began to breathe more easily he sat upright, listening. 'I think we've had a stroke of luck. Sanchez may have hurt the dog too badly for it to be able to track us, but he'll have telephoned for more help and we don't know how near his friends are. Still, we should have an hour or so before they can get here and come after us but we'll have to stay away from any roads. We don't want to walk into his reinforcements when they are coming up to meet him.'

'How do we know which way to go?'

'We go downhill towards the villages in the valley. If we come to a stream we follow it because it will be going towards the sea and all those lovely seaside resorts with policemen. Are you ready to carry on?'

She levered herself to her feet. Now they had put some distance between themselves and the farm they felt able to go more slowly and carefully. After all, as John pointed out, they didn't want to risk falling down some hole and injuring themselves in the dark.

Sometimes they reached an open point where they could look out over the dark hill and gaze eagerly around, but the few faint lights that indicated houses and possible help seemed very far away.

The point came, however, when they were both too exhausted from fighting against the thick thorny undergrowth to go on. They found a corner where a fallen tree gave them something to lean on. The ground was dry, still keeping some hint of the daytime warmth, and they lay down together gratefully.

'We must rest for a while,' John panted.

'John,' Carol said a little uneasily, 'is there any wildlife in these woods?'

'Some,' he said sleepily. 'There are rabbits and foxes, of course, and a few snakes, and there are supposed to be some wild boar somewhere. Don't worry. They won't attack unless you provoke them.'

Soon his regular breathing showed that he was asleep, but Carol lay awake for a while listening anxiously, until she decided that she would rather face a wild boar than Sanchez with his shotgun.

Her scream brought John from his troubled sleep to instant alertness, and he jerked upright and looked around for their enemies. The sun was rising, and by its early light he could see that Carol was looking at him with horror. 'What's the matter?'

'Your hands — and your shirt!'

He looked down and saw that the front of his shirt was torn to ribbons and bloodstained. He lifted his hands and saw that they bore several deep cuts, which had bled profusely. 'It was that wire,' he groaned. 'Those blankets were too thin to cover it properly. I thought I felt it biting into my hands as I pulled myself up, but after that I was too worried about Sanchez coming after us to worry about scratches.'

'Those aren't scratches!' Carol protested as she took his hands and examined them. 'Those cuts need treatment in case they get infected.'

'You came the same way. What about you?'

She checked carefully and found a few tears in her jeans and some cuts on her legs. 'That must have happened when I went over the wall. I haven't come off too badly. You were holding my hands so they were protected.'

He grimaced. 'No wonder I felt sore whenever I moved during the night.' He looked round. The sun was above the horizon. 'We'd better start moving. Sanchez and his friends will be looking for us now.'

He tried to ignore the way the cuts hurt as he moved and they began to make their way down to the valley where they hoped to find safety. Even in daylight it was difficult to make much speed through the woods, but they knew they had to find help soon before the kidnappers tracked them down.

The sun was higher in the sky when they heard dogs barking in the distance. Carol had visions of a whole pack of dogs pursuing them, but John listened carefully and then shook his head. 'Those dogs aren't hunting. They're probably farm dogs, so let's make our way towards them.'

This took another thirty minutes, and then he was proved right when they saw a stone farmhouse with scattered outbuildings next to a road. Carol felt a sudden surge of happiness as the weight of fear was lifted from her. Soon they would return to the normal world and safety.

John was looking at himself and then at Carol, both bloodstained and dressed in ragged, dirty clothes. 'It's a pity we look such sights. The farmer may set the dogs on us.'

'Nonsense! He'll see we need help,' Carol said with blissful certainty.

'Let's be a little cautious and look round before we knock on the door.'

They crouched down and peered out at the farm and saw a woman come out with a basket of clothes and start hanging them on a line. They could hear hens clucking and then the woman shouting at the dogs. It was a reassuringly normal sight.

'It looks all right,' John decided finally. 'Put on your best smile and hope they take pity on us.'

They stood up and had started a vain attempt to brush their clothes down and tidy themselves up when John's head jerked round as he heard the sound of an engine nearing the farm and then stopping. Without warning he pulled Carol to the ground. She protested vigorously, but he clamped a hand over her mouth. 'Quiet! It's the van, the van that took us to the hut! Look!'

Horrified, she cautiously lifted her head. There indeed was the white van, and even as she looked Anna Dreiser got out, followed by a man in black.

'John!'

'I know. I can see her. And the man is her so-called chauffeur. Wait here.' He was carefully making his way closer to the farm as Anna Dreiser and her companion approached the woman in the yard. There was a rapid conversation, and Carol could see the farm-woman nodding rapidly. Then Madam Dreiser and the chauffeur got back into the van and drove on. Soon afterwards John was back with Carol, cursing heartily.

'Forget about approaching this farm or any other on this road! They told the woman that we are relatives of theirs — drug addicts — and that they have been keeping us in a house in the woods and trying to cure our addiction. According to them we attacked the nurse and escaped. They told the woman that we are very dangerous and that if she even thinks she sees us she must telephone them at once. On no account must she let us near her or talk to us.'

They heard the slam of a door and

looked at the farm again. The woman was gone, obviously shutting herself in the safety of the house, and as they watched they saw the shutters being closed. There was no help for them there, and Dreiser and her friends were very near.

7

This last blow, just when help seemed within reach, threatened to be too much for Carol. She wrapped her arms round her knees, rested her head on them and closed her eyes, trying to shut out the world. All the effort of escaping from Sanchez and the time spent fighting their way through the woods had been wasted.

Anna Dreiser was ahead of them, spreading lies about the danger they brought, and as soon as Carol and John approached anyone for help their kidnappers would be informed and they would be recaptured. What was the point of struggling on? If the white van had reappeared at that moment Carol would have walked to it and climbed docilely inside.

John was murmuring encouragement. 'Don't give up! They haven't got us yet!'

She rocked backwards and forwards, refusing to look at him. 'What's the use? Whatever we do, they'll catch us eventually.'

His voice changed. 'Don't be so hopeless! It looks as if your parents were right all along. You're dim and useless!'

She looked up indignantly and caught the worry on his face. She sniffed, wiped the tears away inelegantly with her hand, and sat up. 'All right, I get the message. Can't a girl even feel depressed for a minute? Where can we go?'

He looked relieved at her renewed spirit. 'To a town or a village. Dreiser may persuade isolated farmers to give us up, but if you have a group of people they won't feel so frightened of us and they will ask questions. All we need is the chance to make one phone call to Barcelona.'

Although the woods were not so thick and impenetrable now, Carol and John found it hard to make progress.

Hunger was weakening them and they had had only a few hours rest on the rocky ground. They felt stiff and clumsy and the day was growing hot, and flies were buzzing around the bloodstains on their clothes and they were nearly at the limit of their endurance. They saw two or three isolated settlements but gave them a wide berth.

Carol trudged on stubbornly, one foot in front of the other. Her shoes had been designed for walking in the city and now she was painfully aware of blisters. Then there was the rattle of small stones and a grunt of pain. John had slipped on some loose gravel and fallen heavily. He stood up with difficulty, but winced as he put weight on his right foot.

'I think I've sprained it,' he said through gritted teeth and looked at Carol despairingly.

'If this is the bit where you tell me to save myself and go on without you, forget it!' she snapped. 'Here, I can support you.'

With his arm round her shoulders and hers round his waist, they made progress, but very slowly. The only comfort was that they were gradually nearing the floor of the valley. Once there they could follow down it to the coast, where busy roads and resorts meant contact with the authorities.

They found a footpath too narrow for a car to negotiate and by mutual agreement began to follow it, too tired to make their own way through the trees any longer. It grew a little wider and became a properly surfaced road. On one side there were market gardens and a barn instead of woods, and then they saw houses clustered together. They had come to a village!

Somehow they managed to speed up a little and their aches and pains faded. The village was little more than a hamlet, but at last they reached the paved square that was clearly the centre and stopped, wondering what to do next. The full heat of the midday sun beat down and the square was deserted, its inhabitants obviously sheltering indoors.

Carol gazed at the front doors, wondering which one concealed people who would listen to them and give them aid. Or were the doors shut because Anna Dreiser had been here already and warned the residents of the violent addicts who might threaten them? Would every door remain fastened against them?

Well, they would have to put it to the test soon. John pointed to a building on one side of the square. 'At least there's a café. There's sure to be a telephone there and we have enough cash to pay for a call.'

How sensible and normal! They would ask politely where the telephone was, change John's note into coins, insert the coins, dial the number that would connect them to Isabella Sanchez, and she would do the rest. All they would have to do afterwards would be to sit and wait.

Carol and John were only twenty

yards from the café when they heard a noise and saw the white van enter the square, but John's ankle prevented them running for shelter.

There was a sudden squeal of brakes as the driver stopped abruptly. Anna Dreiser and her companion in black leapt from the van. They were separated from Carol and John only by the width of the small square and Carol saw Anna Dreiser put her hand in her pocket and then saw the sunlight striking on the bright metal of her pistol. The woman stared across at them and deliberately beckoned them to come nearer. The gun aimed steadily at them did away with the need for words.

A little earlier Carol might have obeyed that summons and admitted defeat, but now, having pushed herself to the limit to reach freedom, she was filled with sudden pure fury. She was Carol Oliver, and she would not be dragged ignominiously back to humiliating imprisonment or death.

People must be searching for her, her

name would be known. Somewhere in these silent houses people must be awake and within earshot. She stepped away from John and took a deep breath.

'I am Carol Oliver!' she shouted as loudly as she could, and her name echoed round the square. 'Carol Oliver! Carol Oliver!' she yelled defiantly again and again, and could hear that John was also shouting something now. Maybe it was pointless defiance, maybe Anna Dreiser would simply shoot them both to ensure their silence, but Carol would not surrender.

She became aware that some men had come surging out of the bar and were gazing at the scene in bewilderment. She turned to them, holding out her arms in appeal. 'Help me! I am Carol Oliver!' she demanded as John continued shouting. She whirled round as she heard the van door slam. Faced with an audience, Anna Dreiser and the man in black had retreated to the vehicle, and now the engine burst into life as they drove away at top speed.

A man from the bar had reached her, his face showing wary suspicion as he looked at her and John, and he was saying something in Spanish. John was beside her again, his arm round her shoulders to hold himself upright. Carol faced the villagers with sparkling eyes. She was Carol Oliver and she had faced down her enemies. She had triumphed.

The elation did not last long, however. A small crowd had gathered round the two of them, asking questions, commenting on their appearance and telling each other what had happened. John was apparently explaining their situation. After the isolation of the previous few days it was too much, and Carol put her hands over her ears to shut out the noise.

The man who had reached them first gestured towards the bar and they made their way to it. The door was shut, excluding most of the villagers, and John and Carol sank gratefully down on wooden chairs. A lively discussion broke out between the half-dozen villagers in the café, with John listening intently and occasionally interrupting.

'What are they saying? Why haven't they called Barcelona?' Carol wanted to know.

'They are not sure whether we are telling the truth or whether we are criminals being hunted by another gang. They won't let us make a call in case we are summoning more gun-toting accomplices.'

She stared at him.

'Don't be surprised. Would you unhesitatingly welcome anyone who looked like us? We both look thoroughly villainous, you know.'

He listened again. 'The one thing in our favour is that Dreiser and her friends ran away.'

His face brightened with relief. 'They've decided this is a matter for the police.'

The bar owner was telephoning. 'The police will tell him who we are,' Carol said happily.

'Not necessarily. He's calling a local policeman, a friend, to ask for advice.'

The bar owner replaced the telephone, came to look at them, and clearly came to a decision. He said something in Spanish to Carol.

'He is asking if you want anything,' John translated.

'A cup of coffee,' Carol said with heartfelt sincerity.

The man filled two large cups from the gurgling machine on the counter, put them on a tray, and added some slices of bread and cold potato omelette.

Carol cradled the coffee in her hands, sipping it slowly. When the barman handed John a cup he took it gratefully but winced as his lacerated hands felt the heat from the hot cup and she looked at him anxiously. 'You need a doctor.'

He grinned in spite of his pain. 'First things first. Coffee, food, and the police. Then a little first-aid.'

★ ★ ★

They were not sure how long they would have to wait, but in fact it was less than an hour before a sleek steel-grey limousine, probably the most luxurious car that had ever been seen in the village, came to a halt in front of the bar. It was not alone.

There were two jeeps filled with members of the police, the Guardia Civil, and soon a helicopter was clattering overhead. Every inhabitant of the village was out to witness the invasion. The bar owner eyed his guests with increased respect. Either they were indeed kidnap victims or very important criminals indeed.

John and Carol were waiting at the bar door to greet the new arrivals, and when a tall slender man with grey hair got out of the car Carol ran to meet him and threw her arms around him. He held her to him wordlessly, only releasing her as John approached more slowly.

'You can't imagine how relieved I am to see the two of you,' Mr Oliver began, and then stopped suddenly, appalled, as he surveyed them from head to foot and took in the full details of their dirty, bloodstained bedraggled appearance.

'Don't worry!' Carol assured him hastily. 'We're all right. At least, I am. John has some cuts that need attention.'

'They're nothing to worry about,' John said hastily, 'though I'd rather not shake hands if you don't mind, and Carol's got some scratches as well.'

Mr Oliver was looking thoughtfully at his bloody, filthy, happy only-child. Perhaps there was more to her than he had thought.

John gazed in awe at the armed police busy checking their weapons and spreading out maps. An officer approached the small group, intent on getting information, and Carol and John spent the next few minutes describing Anna Dreiser and Sanchez and telling the officer everything they could remember about the hut and its possible location. When the officer was satisfied that they could do no more to help he went outside and soon the police jeeps were driving off, the helicopter following them.

'Now perhaps we can get you two back to the city and whatever attention you need. My wife and John's parents are already there,' Mr Oliver said briskly.

The bar owner was thanked for his help. The expensive car and the convoy of police and the frenetic activity in the tiny square seemed to have overcome him and he had retreated behind his bar. Now, however, as his guests were ready to leave, he spoke anxiously and at some length to John, who nodded emphatically.

While Mr Oliver's chauffeur drove them back towards Barcelona with unobtrusive skill, the three of them sat in the back. Carol luxuriated in the sensation of sinking into the deep leather cushions, her father's arm round her shoulders.

'When we get back to the hotel,' she said dreamily, 'I'm going to fall flat on one of the big soft beds and go to sleep for hours and hours.'

Her father looked down at her, his nose wrinkling fastidiously. 'May I suggest a bath first? You really need one, my darling.' He turned to John. 'A doctor will be waiting to examine both of you. If I'd known the state you were in, I'd have brought him with me!'

'We'll survive,' said his daughter calmly, then asked what the bar owner was fussing about.

'Oh, that,' said John. 'Well, while you were shouting your name — which was definitely a bright idea — I was shouting something else which I thought might persuade the villagers to take our side.'

'What was it?'

'A big reward if you help us!' he said smugly. 'The bar owner is a practical man and wants to know how much and when they will get it.'

'I'll see to that,' Mr Oliver said with feeling. 'Even if I give them enough to rebuild the entire village, it will still only be a fraction of what the kidnappers were demanding.' He smiled with satisfaction. 'I'm looking forward to telling certain banks that we won't need their money after all.'

'Were their terms hard?' John asked.

'Very. In fact they may be quite disappointed that you've managed to escape before we had to pay up.' He hesitated. 'Though at the time we were quite glad to get a ransom demand. When did you last see your car, John?'

'My car? Well, I drove into the city centre to meet Carol and parked it in some street.' John sat up. 'Was it stolen?'

'That afternoon your secretary got a call from the police to say that your car had been found wrecked in a gully off a minor road near Tarragona. It still had your briefcase in with your name and some letters with the office address. She knew that you had been going to meet Carol, contacted me, and we thought the two of you had had a road accident and had been carted off to hospital somewhere. Then a certain Anna Dreiser telephoned and we found out what had really happened to you.'

Already they were on the busy coast road that ran from France to Barcelona. Lorries thundered past them and the sea glittered on their left beyond the clusters of tall hotels that marked the various resorts where the busy summer season was now under way. Carol, drowsily content in the great car, had a brief mental vision of the infinite variety of Spain.

Soon they were on the outskirts of Barcelona and the driver was soon threading his way through the dense city traffic, and at last they were at the world-famous hotel and being smoothly whisked up to their families' suites.

Mrs Oliver took one look at Carol, greeted her with suitable warmth, and then went into action. She and her maid stripped Carol and threw away her ruined clothing. In five minutes they had Carol in the hot, expensively-scented bath of which she had dreamed. She lay back and closed her eyes, letting the dirt and the tension soak away. Then Carol was wrapped in towels and dried like a child, her eyes already closing with fatigue.

Finally she was ready to climb into bed, but before she was allowed to go to sleep the doctor that her father had mentioned appeared to give her a brief check, examining the cuts on her legs and pronouncing them superficial. At last she was alone, and she was asleep before the door had even closed softly behind her mother.

She woke twelve hours later. At first she did not know where she was and sat up in panic, only to relax as she saw her mother's elegant figure sitting in a chair leafing through a fashion magazine by the light of a discreet lamp. When she saw that her daughter was awake, Mrs Oliver walked over to the window and pulled the curtains. Barcelona's sunlit roofscape was visible outside.

'You've woken up to a beautiful morning,' Mrs Oliver observed. 'How are you?'

'Fine,' Carol said automatically, and then moved. 'Oh! No, I'm not! My legs and feet are sore and I ache all over!'

'The doctor said that is only to be expected,' her mother said. 'He did point out that you had a large number of bruises as well as the cuts on your legs and the blisters on your feet. Nothing serious.'

'I suppose I got them when we fell over the wall,' Carol said, moving gingerly. 'And there were all the times I fell down in the woods.' She managed to achieve a moderately comfortable position and looked up at her mother. 'I do feel very hungry, Mother.'

'Breakfast will be here as soon as you've washed,' her mother said calmly.

Carol, obediently shuffling to the bathroom like an old woman, reflected while she washed briefly and brushed her teeth that, although she sometimes wished for more signs of affection from her mother, it was very soothing to have a parent who didn't fuss over you.

Breakfast was light and digestible.

Apparently this was what the doctor had recommended. Carol ate it all and looked sadly at the empty plate, promising herself frequent snacks later.

'Your father has told me everything that you told him yesterday, but he thought you might like to tell me all the details,' Mrs Oliver said, obedient to her husband's instructions to get as much information as possible.

So Carol told her of the hours in the hut, hours that were already beginning to seem like a bad dream. Her mother shuddered at her account. She also questioned Carol closely about John's behaviour during their captivity.

'He was marvellous!' Carol told her. 'He was so practical, and he was the one who kept the meat for the dog so we could escape!'

Her mother was looking thoughtful. 'I always thought him a rather conceited young man, but I may have misjudged him.'

'No, he's not at all conceited,' Carol

said emphatically. 'He is very under-standing, and he helped me to understand myself as well.'

'Really?'

But Carol was silent. This was not the time to tell her mother that her daughter planned to take over her own life in future.

8

Carol thought the ordeal was over, but of course it was not as simple as that. The police wanted as much information as possible, and that afternoon Carol put on a light dress and flat shoes that were kind to her still painful feet, and went through to the suite's lounge, where she was delighted to find John waiting for her as well as her father and two men in dark suits.

She held out her hands to greet him, but he shook his head. Bundles of white bandages emerged from the sleeves of his sweatshirt. 'The doctor decided one or two cuts were getting infected,' he said in disgusted tones. 'As a result, I can't even feed myself!'

'And your chest?'

'Under this shirt I look like a mummy!'

One of the men with him coughed

politely to draw attention to the fact that they had more important matters to discuss. 'If we could sit down?' he said, in tones which implied that he was more used to giving orders than being carefully polite, and then he gave them the latest news.

'I am afraid that the woman who called herself Anna Dreiser and her accomplice escaped. The van was found abandoned a few miles from the village. They must have had someone waiting for them and been miles away before we got there.'

'Did you find the farm? Was Sanchez there?'

'We found the farm without too much trouble. The dog you told us about was there, killed by a shotgun.' His gaze fell. 'Sanchez was there too. He had been killed by a pistol-shot. I do not think that gang forgive weaknesses.'

Now the second man was opening a briefcase and taking out some large flat books. Opened, they proved to be full of photographs which Carol and John studied obediently until Carol pointed at one picture. 'That's Sanchez!'

The policeman nodded approval. 'Correct. He was already known to the police for crimes of violence, though as far as we know he had not been involved in kidnapping before. We suspect he was a local recruit, employed because of his knowledge of the area.'

Another book was brought out, and Carol noticed that they were being watched carefully as this one was examined.

She hesitated over one face, frowning, decided she did not know it, and started to turn the page.

'Wait, Carol! Let me have another look.'

John was staring at the same face. 'I think that was the chauffeur,' he said quietly.

Carol pursed her lips. 'I don't think so. This man is blond, and the chauffeur had dark hair.'

John covered up the top of the

photograph with his bandaged hand. 'Look again. Look at the features.'

This time the face did look more familiar. 'You may be right,' she said slowly.

The policeman relaxed slightly, as though they had passed some important test. 'Do you recognise anybody else?'

A few pages later both John and Carol were unanimous. 'That's Anna Dreiser!'

Both policemen looked highly satisfied as the books were put away. John wanted to know more. 'Who were those two? Have they kidnapped anyone else?'

'Perhaps. If so, it is not their main activity.' He leaned back and sighed. 'The past few years have seen great upheavals in some parts of the world. The collapse of Communism in Russia and the break-up of Yugoslavia have given rise to the growth of ruthless, violent groups who now use the skills they learned during the disturbances for their own private end.

'Many genuinely believe in the cause for which they fight, but others see it as a chance to make money from the distress of their countries. The pair you knew as the chauffeur, and Anna Dreiser are among the latter. They have extorted money from people, sold arms to opposing sides and indulged in armed robbery. They are very dangerous indeed.'

He looked at them questioningly. 'Have you any idea how they identified you as a suitable target, Miss Oliver?'

Resignedly, Carol told them about Juan, and saw how her father's lips tightened. She felt as if she were talking about a much younger, naïve girl than she was now, and wondered how she could have been so stupid.

The policeman noted the facts but made no comment. Later they learned that he had been to the bar, but Juan's cousin had said that he knew nothing of Juan's plans and that the young man had vanished a couple of days earlier. He had assumed he had got another job in a yacht.

'I'll be glad to get back to the world of finance and office politics,' John said with feeling. 'If I'd known the kind of people we were dealing with I would have been even more terrified.'

At least he had his work to return to, Carol found herself thinking enviously a few days later. Life returned to normal surprisingly quickly once the initial excitement of their disappearance and return had worn off. Mr Oliver joined John at the Barcelona office, while the Oldfields returned to London. Mrs Oliver was busy socialising and shopping, and Carol felt very much at a loose end.

She was wondering what to do with herself one morning when her father sought her out and told her that it had been agreed that she and her mother should go on a month-long cruise. 'It will help you recover from your ordeal,' he explained.

'You mean it will get me out of the way for a few weeks,' she retorted.

It was the first time that she had not

fallen in meekly with her father's wishes, and Mr Oliver stared. 'What do you mean?'

It was too late to go back. 'I mean that once again you are treating me like a parcel with no wishes of my own. You're bundling me off on a cruise and when I come back you'll think of somewhere else to send me. Why not ask me what I want to do?'

'Because when you did what you wanted, you fell for some worthless youth and ended up being kidnapped,' he pointed out cuttingly.

'Are you surprised? I'm hopelessly ignorant of what's needed for self-preservation because I've never had a chance to learn from experience. It was all right to protect me from the world when I was a child, Father, but I'm growing up.'

He sat down and looked at her steadily. 'What do you want to do?'

She took a deep breath, trying to recall what she had said to John. 'I want to go to college. I think I should take a general course at first to find out what interests me most, and then I can specialise.'

'You would be mixing with students. There would be nobody of your own kind and you would be very lonely.'

'I'd be a student as well. I could make friends. That would be as important as studying.'

'It's out of the question, Carol. Your mother and I couldn't leave you in London on your own when we are away on business.' He spoke so decisively that that seemed to be the end of the matter, but Carol grabbed desperately at one last straw.

'John said his mother would let me live with her and his sisters!'

Her father looked at his watch and stood up. 'We'll talk about it some other time,' he said.

Carol doubted if that time would ever come, and was still simmering about what she saw as the unfeeling dismissal of her wishes, when John came to collect her the following day.

Carol's belongings had been collected from the proprietress of the *hostal* where Carol had been staying before her abduction, but she wanted to apologise for the trouble she had caused the lady, and this required John as interpreter. It was the first opportunity they had had to go together.

The lift was apparently not working, but when they had climbed the stairs the señora flung her arms around them, greeted them with kisses, and gave a dramatic display of mime that conveyed her fear when Carol failed to return, the suspense, and her delight at the safe ending of the story. Carol thanked her shyly in English and John in his fluent Spanish.

Back on the street, John looked around. 'What shall we do now? It's too late to go back to the office.'

'Coffee?' Carol suggested.

He grimaced. 'If we go back to the usual place, do you promise you won't speak to any strangers?'

They settled at a table and ordered

coffee. Carol looked round, remembering all that had happened since she last sat here. John's hands were still heavily plastered but the bandages had been removed and he had little difficulty with his cup.

Carol gazed at the crowded square with the fountains forming a glistening cascade in the sunlight. 'I thought I would be frightened to walk through Barcelona and come back here, but in fact I feel perfectly all right.'

'Perhaps it's because we escaped and beat the kidnappers. We feel we've won.'

Carol shuddered. 'I wouldn't go that far. After all, they're still free and I won't feel we've won till they've been caught.'

'I think I feel a little that way, but they could have gone anywhere in Europe. We'll probably never hear anything about them again. Once we've dealt with all the matters arising we should try to put the whole thing behind us.'

'Matters arising?'

'Things like thanking the lady just now, and seeing that Isabella Sanchez gets an enormous bonus. She was acting as the centre of communication for our families and the police. She virtually never left the office in case there was some emergency call.'

Carol raised her eyebrows speculatively. 'Going by everything you've told me, is it possible that Miss Sanchez had a weakness for you?'

'Definitely not! You should see the handsome chap she's engaged to. However, Isabella is ambitious, and her work during the crisis will be remembered. She'll get a marvellous reference if she ever leaves the firm, you can be sure of that.'

'What are we going to do about your promise of 'a big reward' to the village? Isn't that one of the matters arising?'

'Indeed it is and I hadn't forgotten. When I was trying to find out what would benefit them all the most I discovered that the village's water system was inadequate for modern needs. In the next few months the system will be greatly improved.'

Carol sighed with pleasure and relaxed. 'You seem to have sorted everything out, even though it was all my fault, of course.'

'You might have been more careful if you hadn't been so coddled and protected all your life.'

'That's what I said to my father,' she said mournfully and told him about her conversation with him. 'The only time when he seemed to weaken a little was when I said that your family could keep an eye on me.'

John slanted a rather odd look at her. 'Do you realise that your mother thinks you should get married, and that I'm her first choice?'

Carol spilled her coffee.

'I'm deadly serious,' he went on. 'According to my mother, as far as she is concerned, it is the perfect solution. Your parents can't think what to do with you, and as they always expected you to marry some prosperous young businessman and start being a good wife, your mother thinks marriage to me will solve the problem.'

'But I don't want to marry you!'

'Thank you very much,' he said equably.

'You know what I mean. I've met you half-a-dozen times in my life socially and I've been held prisoner in a hut with you, but that's not exactly the perfect basis for marriage, is it? Anyway, I don't want a husband who snores and you do.'

He shook with laughter. 'Please don't go around telling people that, Carol.' He sobered and patted her hand. 'It's all right. I understand perfectly how you feel, and I feel the same way about you. After what we've been through together, I like you and I know we will be friends in the future, but I hope that marriage will involve love and romance, and there has certainly been none of that between the two of us.'

Carol brooded for a while on what he had said. Was John good husband material? Obviously. He was wealthy, intelligent, and reasonably good-looking, an eminently acceptable suitor. Anyway, she was certain that for her he would always be a very good friend, but nothing more.

9

'Time for one last stroll down Las Ramblas,' John announced. He held out his hand to Carol. 'Come on. Forget our families and that horrible time in the hut. Let's just be a boy and a girl enjoying one of the most exciting cities in the world.'

So they started their walk along that unique Spanish street. John was still limping slightly, but his ankle no longer hurt.

As usual Las Ramblas was crowded with Spaniards who were pleasantly engaged in meeting their friends or having a few drinks while they decided what to do with the rest of an evening that could last into the small hours of the night.

While John inspected a display of magazines, Carol idly watched the passers-by and found herself following the progress of one woman who was walking through the crowds on her own.

Suddenly Carol's gaze grew fixed. Her grip on John's hand tightened convulsively until he gave a cry of pain and snatched his hand away. She turned to him, wild-eyed. 'Look! Look at that woman!'

Nursing his hand tenderly, John stared after the solitary walker. He saw the back of a drably-dressed woman with straggly dark hair touched with grey.

'I've never seen her before in my life.'

'You have! Of course you have! That's Anna Dreiser!'

He looked again at the woman who had been forced to stop at the edge of the road by the stream of traffic. 'It's nothing like her. Anna Dreiser was a blonde, smartly dressed!'

Carol was holding his sleeve, pulling him after the woman. 'She's changed her clothes and her hair colour, but that is Anna Dreiser. I recognised the way she walked and the shape of her head.'

The woman looked impatiently from side to side as she waited for an opportunity to cross the road, and for a moment her profile was silhouetted against the light of a shop front. John stared incredulously. 'You're right,' he said, almost unable to believe his eyes. 'It is her, but what can we do?'

'We can't let her get away. Let's follow her.'

They were a few yards behind the woman when she finally crossed to the opposite pavement and went through an archway into the square beyond. John extracted his mobile phone from his pocket and rapidly keyed in a number. 'I'm calling the police,' he explained quietly. 'They can get hold of the Inspector who came to see us. I just hope he hasn't finished work for the night.'

John hastily explained the position as he and Carol unobtrusively tracked the woman across the square, then nodded and said, 'yes,' several times as he listened to the response.

'They're trying to contact the Inspector, then they can get a special squad to us within ten minutes. I'll call them back to tell them where she's heading.'

Carol was still clutching him, watching the woman's slow progress through the crowd with a growing excitement. Now she and John were the hunters and the woman was their prey. Now was their chance to get their revenge for what she had made them suffer.

'Tell them to get here as soon as possible. She's a murderess as well as a kidnapper. I want her caught and punished for what she did to us and to Sanchez.'

John slipped his free arm round her and she rested her head on his shoulder for a second, finding it strangely comforting. 'I feel exactly the same. Now, let's be ever so casual, but make sure we keep her within sight.'

This was easy when Anna Dreiser was in the square, and the brightly-lit streets around it, but when she moved off into the narrow back streets it became more difficult.

John looked at his watch. 'If we can follow her for another two minutes the police should be here.'

Anna Dreiser turned a corner into a narrow passageway. John and Carol stopped to peer at the battered sign on the wall.

'I'll just call the police to give them the name of this street,' John decided, taking out his mobile again, but before he could key in the number a hand snaked round from behind him and closed over the mobile, snatching it from him. At the same time Carol found herself struggling with a man who had seized her from behind.

She saw John turn to face the man who had taken his mobile, only to find himself looking at a revolver held by the so-called chauffeur. The man gestured down the passageway. 'Follow the lady,' he ordered.

John hesitated, but the other man was already half-carrying, half-dragging

Carol into the entrance. With the gun threatening him, John had no choice but to obey. They were pulled and pushed a few yards along the narrow alley and then into an unlit doorway. They stumbled up some steep stairs, still in darkness, and then suddenly saw a gleam of light as a door opened ahead of them and they heard Anna Dreiser's voice challenging the newcomers.

The chauffeur spat out a brief response, then Carol felt a hand shove her forward and she almost fell into the lighted room. The others followed and the door was slammed shut behind them.

They were in a small bare room lit by a weak electric light bulb which showed wallpaper falling off rotten plaster and a window which had been boarded up. The only furniture was a chair and a rickety table.

'We saw these two following you, so we waited till they were nearly here and then grabbed them,' said the chauffeur, grinning widely.

John and Carol stood defiantly side by side.

Anna Dreiser stared at the two prisoners, then looked at their captives with fury. 'Why have you brought them here? You could have knocked them out somewhere. We're clearing out in a few minutes!'

The man was taken aback. 'Can't we take them with us?'

'Out of the question!' Then she looked at John and Carol again, and there was a gleam of malicious triumph in her eyes. 'On the other hand, I suppose this is a delightful surprise! A leaving present from Barcelona. A chance to pay the two of you back for the trouble you have caused us! Don't bother screaming for help. The building is empty, due to be demolished soon, and there is no-one around to hear you.'

The chauffeur took John's mobile phone from his jacket. 'The man was using this, probably to alert the police. We'll have to get out of here very quickly.'

Anna Dreiser almost snarled, and

then shrugged her shoulders. 'It takes time to search even a few streets in this rabbit warren. We can be clear in plenty of time, but these two stay here.' There was a flat finality in her tone, which made Carol feel as if she had turned to stone.

'But they're worth a lot of money! Are you sure we can't take them?'

Anna Dreiser shook her head. 'We can't take the risk. Nothing must go wrong in the next few hours. Dragging two people along would put everything in danger. It's a pity, I know, but there is no alternative.'

The chauffeur was about to protest and the other man was also frowning. The prisoners were momentarily ignored, and John seized the chance to lash out at the two men, hoping to give Carol a chance to escape. He had underestimated the speed and strength of the two, however, and received a blow on the chest which landed full on the half-healed cuts caused by the wire. He almost fainted with the pain and could offer no resistance as he was hauled up and dumped on the chair.

'Tie him up before he causes any more trouble,' Anna Dreiser ordered, and Carol could only watch as his hands were tied behind him and fastened to the chair back. She felt faintly sick, but stared defiantly at the other woman, who looked her up and down, sneering.

'You needn't bother to tie up this little thing,' Anna Dreiser told her two accomplices when they turned towards Carol. 'She's too feeble to cause me any trouble.'

Carol stood in silent humiliation as Anna Dreiser ignored the prisoners while she issued orders to the two men. 'You two go now. You know what you have to do?'

The men nodded, and she gave a satisfied smile. 'I will meet you at the rendezvous in exactly two hours' time. By ten tomorrow the three of us will be safely aboard a ship on our way to

South America. Now hurry, unless you want to walk into the arms of the police! I'll leave as soon as I've dealt with these two.'

She drew a small gun from her pocket. The men left quickly and quietly, and Anna Dreiser turned to Carol and John.

'Let Carol go!' John begged hopelessly, but the woman shook her head.

'The silly little girl has already caused more than enough trouble.'

Afterwards Carol decided that it was the patronising note in Anna Dreiser's voice which brought her simmering anger to boiling point. She had been feeling futile and stupid, even guilty at having once again led John as well as herself into the power of these people. This last insult drove her into action.

She flung herself at the woman before Anna Dreiser could bring the gun round towards her, knocking her to the floor. Surprise had given her an advantage, but then the older, bigger woman recovered and Carol found that she was no match for an opponent obviously trained to fight hand-to-hand.

She was soon on the defensive, trying to shield herself from blows as Anna Dreiser used the gun to hit her. Then Carol lashed out in one final last despairing attempt, a lucky blow which knocked the gun from the woman's hand so that it skittered across the floor and under the chair to which John was tied.

Anna Dreiser dived to recover it, but John was kicking out at the gun, trying to keep it out of her reach. It slid across the floor again, and this time Carol desperately clawed out and seized it.

Carol scrambled up holding the gun, her heart pounding. She hadn't the slightest idea how to use it. Didn't you have to release a safety catch? Where was that? Anna Dreiser was on her feet now, looking warily at Carol, and then, as she sensed the girl's bewilderment, she moved cautiously towards her.

'Run, Carol!' John shouted. 'Go! Get help!'

How could she leave him there? But

if Anna snatched the gun from her she would kill both of them. Carol turned, tore the door open, and fled down the stairs.

It was like her worst nightmares. She was lost in a dark maze of streets, and within seconds she could hear Anna Dreiser pounding after her. She ran recklessly at top speed, hoping that no unseen obstacle would trip her. In this populous city it seemed that no-one else had ventured among these abandoned streets.

She would not be hunted down like a frightened animal, though. Suddenly, as they reached an open space where several alleys met, she whirled round and stood, legs apart, holding the gun in both hands. Instinctively she was copying a posture she had seen a hundred times on films, but it was convincing enough to bring Anna Dreiser to a halt.

'Don't be silly,' the older woman said, panting, carefully eyeing the gun and gradually edging closer. 'You can't shoot me. You don't know how to use a gun.'

'Perhaps I'll be lucky,' Carol said wildly.

Her opponent laughed. 'You daren't. You're a silly little girl, and you're too scared.'

'But we are not, señora.' It was a man's voice, calm and authoritative, and even as he spoke men in uniform appeared out of the alleyways, guns glinting in their hands, all of them aimed at Anna Dreiser, who stared round wildly, looking for a way of escape. As they came towards her she took one step backwards, then another, and then turned and ran into the darkness. There was the sound of shots, but no scream, and Carol saw some of the men racing in pursuit.

Suddenly the policeman who had interrogated John and herself was by her side, gently taking the gun from her shaking fingers.

Together with some of the police, Carol retraced the path of her frantic flight, and after one or two false turns she recognised the house, its door still wide open. 'He's in there,' she said, and the police moved forward but she did not see them go. The Inspector caught her as she fainted for the first time in her life.

When she came round she was in the back seat of a police car. In the front a policeman dealt with radios crackling with static and urgent Spanish. She pulled herself upright and leant forward.

The policeman turned round and smiled briefly, nodding. 'Don't worry. We have your friend.'

Carol saw a trio of dark figures approaching. John was being partly supported by police officers who helped him into the car beside Carol. She saw the relief on his face. 'They told me you were safe!' he exclaimed thankfully.

She was so happy that she threw her arms around him and hugged him, only to draw back rapidly as he yelped. 'All those cuts seem to have reopened, and when that woman knocked the chair over I hit my head on the floor and was unconscious for a bit so I think I've got a good collection of bruises as well! Did they get Anna Dreiser?'

'I don't think so.'

She couldn't have escaped for a second time! But as the policemen gradually returned in twos and threes, their despondency showed that this was in fact the case. Finally, the leader returned and climbed into the car.

'She got away somewhere in this warren,' he told them sombrely. 'However, she's not out of Barcelona yet. Meanwhile we'd better get you two checked over.'

A doctor inspected Carol at the police station and pronounced her unharmed, and then a policewoman asked if she would like to rest, but Carol shook her head firmly. 'Where's John Oldfield? I want to see how he is.'

She persisted, in spite of the policewoman's soothing assurances that everything was all right, and eventually she was taken along the corridor to an identical room where the doctor was applying fresh dressings to John's chest.

John grinned at her wearily. 'You look as if you might live.'

'What about you?' she enquired, looking at the bloodstained bandages that had been removed.

'This type of thing isn't supposed to happen to respectable accountants! But if I rest for a month, don't move, and don't try to fight any more kidnappers, then I think I'll survive.'

'I hear the doctor is of the same opinion,' said the Inspector calmly, as he came in, followed by another man with a notebook. He shook his head resignedly as they looked at him eagerly. 'There is no sign of the woman and her accomplices so far. We shall be most grateful if you can describe how they look now and how they are dressed.'

Carol concentrated on what had passed in that decrepit room, but all she could remember was her feeling of helplessness as Anna Dreiser spoke to the two men. She shook her head.

'There was something about a ship,' John said hesitantly.

Carol lifted her head triumphantly. 'She said that by ten tomorrow they would be safe on a ship to South America!'

Everything seemed like an anti-climax after that. Carol and John stayed in the nondescript little room.

'I wonder if anyone has contacted my parents?' Carol said finally.

John looked at her in blank horror. 'They'll be worried sick!' He groaned. 'How do we tell them that we've just been kidnapped for the second time?'

A policewoman was hurriedly persuaded to take them to a telephone. When Carol rang the hotel her mother was almost hysterical. 'You didn't say where you were going, and there have been no messages. Where are you?'

'At a police station,' Carol informed her, and bit her lip as she heard the explosion of words at the other end of the line. 'We're all right, honestly. Well, I am, but John could be better.'

Her father obviously took over at this point for she heard his carefully controlled voice. 'Which police station? Why are you there?'

'We were kidnapped again,' Carol said, and suddenly got an urge to laugh hysterically. 'We've been helping the police with their enquiries.'

John, standing by her, gave her a startled glance and seized the telephone. 'We are all right, sir. Could you come and collect us — again?'

Mr Oliver was there in ten minutes.

The next morning Carol had showered and dressed rapidly and was having breakfast when John appeared, heavy-eyed but smiling. 'I've heard from the police. They picked up Anna Dreiser and her companions at the docks.'

She sighed with relief. 'So we have beaten Anna Dreiser in the end.'

They heard no more, and gradually came to realise that they never would.

They had played their part and the secret world they had stumbled upon would now forget them.

The Oldfields reappeared, grimly determined to take their son home and keep him there until he was completely recovered, but he insisted he had to stay in Barcelona long enough to finish his work.

Carol was increasingly restless. Her father had said nothing more about her wish to go to college, but she was aware that her relationship with her mother had altered.

Her mother was regarding her uncertainly, unsure how to treat a daughter who had survived such wild adventures and obviously could no longer be treated as a child.

Then Mr Oliver sought Carol out as she sat reading one morning. 'Your mother and I have been discussing the future.' Carol saw a rare smile twitch the corner of his mouth. 'You have surprised us,' her father continued. 'You've always been a quiet, docile child, and I suppose we thought you would go on like that. It was our fault, we took you for granted a little too much. You'd better look through these brochures for colleges and decide which one you'd prefer. Mrs Oldfield has said that you can stay with her during term time.'

Carol sat up, her face radiant, but her father brushed her thanks aside.

'Both you and John are starting new lives. He has told his father that he wants to work for another firm, to widen his experience. It might be a good idea, but we'll want him back eventually.'

★   ★   ★

Later that day John himself appeared. 'We are definitely flying back to England tomorrow, so let's go for a last look at Barcelona.'

They made their way to a small park, and told each other of their plans for the future. John had already contacted a firm in London which he knew was interested in him. 'How do you feel now you are getting your own way?' John asked Carol.

'Well, at first I felt on top of the world, sure everything would be all right. Now? Now I'm beginning to have doubts. Suppose I can't manage my life by myself? Suppose I'm too dim to be a good student? I'm not sure I can explain.'

'No need to explain. I feel exactly the same. I was so pleased with myself when I'd arranged an interview with this firm, and ten minutes later I decided that I was a fool to give up a job like mine, just because of some stupid idea of proving myself. Still, if the two of us can survive being kidnapped and threatened with murder, surely we can survive any little difficulties at work or college.'

'At least we'll both be in London so we can see each other. We know we can be totally honest with each other.'

John took her hand. 'It will be good

to have a friend like you near me when I need one.'

They smiled at each other, excited at the thought of the future, pleased that they would face it together.

They wandered back to the hotel. Mr Oliver and Mr Oldfield saw them in the entrance hall, still deep in conversation, apparently unaware that they were still holding hands.

'John says he sees her just as a friend,' Mr Oldfield commented.

'Carol says the same about him.'

'I think we'll be planning their wedding within two years,' Mr Oliver said.

Mr Oldfield smiled. 'My wife says one year, and I agree.'

THE END

We do hope that you have enjoyed reading this large print book.

Did you know that all of our titles are available for purchase?

We publish a wide range of high quality large print books including:
Romances, Mysteries, Classics
General Fiction
Non Fiction and Westerns

Special interest titles available in large print are:
The Little Oxford Dictionary
Music Book, Song Book
Hymn Book, Service Book

Also available from us courtesy of Oxford University Press:
Young Readers' Dictionary
(large print edition)
Young Readers' Thesaurus
(large print edition)

For further information or a free brochure, please contact us at:
Ulverscroft Large Print Books Ltd.,
The Green, Bradgate Road, Anstey,
Leicester, LE7 7FU, England.
Tel: (00 44) **0116 236 4325**
Fax: (00 44) **0116 234 0205**

YESTERDAY'S LOVE

Stella Ross

Jessica's return from Africa to claim her inheritance of 'Simon's Cottage', and take up medicine in her home town, is the signal for her past to catch up with her. She had thought the short affair she'd had with her cousin Kirk twelve years ago a long-forgotten incident. But Kirk's unexpected return to England, on a last-hope mission to save his dying son, sparks off nostalgia. It leads Jessica to rethink her life and where it is leading.

THE DOCTOR WAS A DOLL

Claire Vernon

Jackie runs a riding-school and, living happily with her father, feels no desire to get married. When Dr. Simon Hanson comes to the town, Jackie's friends try to matchmake, but he, like Jackie, wishes to remain single and they become good friends. When Jackie's father decides to remarry, she feels she is left all alone, not knowing the happiness that is waiting around the corner.

TO BE WITH YOU

Audrey Weigh

Heather, the proud owner of a small bus line, loves the countryside in her corner of Tasmania. Her life begins to change when two new men move into the area. Colin's charm overcomes her first resistance, while Grant also proves a warmer person than expected. But Colin is jealous when Grant gains special attention. The final test comes with the prospect of living in Hobart. Could Heather bear to leave her home and her business to be with the man she loves?

RUNAWAY HEART

Shirley Allen

Manuella's grandfather intends to marry her to the odious Don Miguel, and persuades her father to agree to the match. In desperation, Manuella, who is half-gypsy, runs away to her other family. When the gypsy camp is attacked by Don Miguel, her father and their followers, she is rescued by two Englishmen, Jonathan Wilde and Roderick Maine. Manuella falls in love with Roderick — but will he consider her suitable to be his wife?

WEB OF DECEIT

Margaret McDonagh

A good-looking man turned up on Louise's doorstep one day, introducing himself as Daniel Kinsella, an Australian friend of her brother-in-law, Greg. He said he had come to stay whilst he did some research — apparently Greg had written to her about it. Louise's initial reaction was to turn him away, but he was very persuasive. However, she was to discover that Daniel had bluffed his way into her life, and soon she found herself caught up in his dangerous mission.